SEA DOGS (AND A CAT)

SEA DOGS

(AND A CAT)

Written and Illustrated
By Susan W. Lyons

SL
SOLO

Sea Dogs (and a Cat)

 Email address: swl1948@msn.com.

ISBN-13: 978-1500769031
ISBN-10: 1500769037
First Edition, September 2014

Dedication

I dedicate this story to my grandchildren, all of whom bring me much joy and happiness. To my children, who have given so much meaning to my life, I thank you. And to my mother and father, who gave me a wonderful childhood, I am eternally grateful.

Acknowledgements

I want to thank my husband, John, for letting me dominate the computer and shut the door to the outside world while I work. He has always supported my creative endeavors. My sisters and brother have, too, so thank you to them. I also want to thank my writing friends, Cynthia and Sheila, for helping me with every stage of my story. All the lovely animals I have known helped me create my characters, so I have to thank them as well.

SL
SPIKE

Chapter One—Solo Hears the Call

By the light of the moon, Solo could see down the hill beyond the front gate and past the apple orchard, almost to the sea. The air was still, so the small black-and-tan dog clearly heard the howl rising from Spyglass Cove. His ears perked up with interest. He didn't recognize the voice. A strange dog was in the area. What could it mean?

Solo never minded spending a summer's night in his doghouse, though it was supposed to be punishment. Usually the nighttime was calm and quiet. He could think about his life as he listened to the crickets chirping in the tall grasses or watched the barn owl coast by overhead. Tonight, however, the routine was broken because of the unusual howling. Solo's heart beat a little faster when he heard it again.

"Aooooh! Yip! Yip! Yip!"

The plaintive, melancholy sound was obviously a distress signal of some kind. He lifted his ears to listen for more.

"Rowf! Rowf!" An answering call! Solo strained to hear more clearly. This voice sounded like Spike's, but not exactly. It was accented and more gruff than usual.

Spike was his new friend, a large spotted Pointer mix that moved to the neighboring farm only last month. Solo had met him in the hayfield one day. After they had growled and strutted in front of each other, someone had suddenly wagged. They couldn't remember who had done it first, but it didn't matter now. They were pals.

"That must be Spike," Solo said aloud. "But what's with the funny language?"

The howling and the answering yelps continued. Solo decided to investigate. He rose on his stubby legs and stretched, then trotted down the path to the front gate. "I'm glad Beth didn't tie me," he thought. He smiled when he remembered her patting his back and tossing the tie out chain aside.

The wooden gate loomed ahead like a solemn white ghost. The fence on either side was choked with overgrown privet hedge, and it was one of Solo's favorite hangouts. It was a great place to lie in wait and surprise passers-by or pesky cats.

He pushed the gate open and passed through when he heard the familiar jingle of a collar. A brown-and-white dog trotted up the path. It was Spike all right, and he was on a mission.

Spike trotted briskly. When he stopped and lifted his muzzle to the sky, Solo thought how fine his friend looked. Spike stood erect, the moonlight making his white fur luminous.

“Halloooo,”Solo called.

Spike turned his head. “Solo? That you, old boy? What are you doing out tonight?”

“Nothing, really. I heard that call from the cove and wondered what was going on.”

“Sounds like an old friend of mine, asking for help.”

“Really?” Now Solo was on full alert.

“Oh, I can’t say yet, but I’m dead certain that’s Captain Rollo, and he’s howling an invitation. Let’s go find out more.”

Solo’s thoughts darted back to his safe, dry doghouse, and to Beth. He was kind of in trouble already. If he wasn’t here in the morning … Swallowing his uneasiness, he answered, “Well, okay.”

“First, I’m going to check out— what was that?” Spike yelped, jumping with all four feet. “I heard something rustling in the hedge.”

S
MITTENS

Chapter Two—Enter the Cat

The large spotted dog and his small, fuzzy friend crept toward the fence. Solo lunged, sticking his nose in the bushes right where the sound had been. A menacing growl escaped from his throat.

Then a small cat darted into view, a hissing, spitting fur ball.

As she shot past Spike, he thrust out a paw and pinned her in place by her tail. She clawed at him but he just laughed. Spike cocked his head at Solo. "We got her."

"Why do we *want* her?" asked Solo, frowning.

"Let go of me, you bully. Let me go!" Her voice hissed as she batted at his leg. Her sharp claws glinted in the moonlight.

Solo put his face close to hers. "Why were you spying on us, you little pest? You should be in the house."

"I have as much right as you do to roam about at night. You don't own the hedge or the farm. My family lived here long before you showed up, so don't get bossy with me." She licked a paw disdainfully.

"Feisty little feline, isn't she?" Spike chuckled again as he released her. Mittens curled her tail toward her body, inspecting it for any damage.

"Mittens always prowls around like she owns the place. She needs to mind her own business."

"Well, I *do* own the place—more than you do, you mongrel. I can trace my bloodline. My family has been here for generations."

"Only because you cats have kittens every few months," Solo sneered.

"Easy, easy." Spike intervened.

"You'd better go home, Mittens," Solo continued. "We are going to the beach to find out what all that howling is about." He dodged the claws that flashed by his face. "Everybody knows that cats hate water. Plus, a seafaring dog is down there and he no doubt hates cats."

"I'm not afraid, so don't try to make me, SO-LO!" Mittens hissed. She twitched her tail and strolled back to the hedge. Sitting on her haunches and jutting her chin out, she added, "I'll do as I please."

Solo shrugged. “Have it your way. Let’s go, Spike. We’re wasting time.”

The two friends crossed the road and found the footpath through the orchard. It led to the shortcut. Once they wound down the rocky pathway, they’d reach the cove in minutes.

The small cat watched them growing smaller as they moved farther and farther away. The moon was bright, so she could see all the way to the cliff’s edge. As the dogs descended and their tails disappeared from view, Mittens followed. She stepped silently, as cats do. She held her own tail high. Her whiskers were stiff with excitement. If there was going to be an adventure, she was ready for it!

SL
CAPTAIN ROLLO

Chapter Three—A Ship, a Fire, and a Surprise

As the three animals trailed down the rocky pathway (one well behind the first two), they could see a bonfire on the sandy beach below. Near the shore, a small boat rocked gently in the waves, and further out a larger ship lay anchored in the bay. Figures of varying sizes moved around the fire. The crackle and pop of burning wood could be heard by the three of them as they drew closer.

Solo wondered about the figures. They were dogs, for sure, but they walked on their two back legs. It looked very weird. Some dogs lifted chunks of driftwood and tossed them on the flames. Another stirred a big kettle at the edge of the bonfire. Yet another lifted a mug to his muzzle and drank like a human!

"Spike, do you see that?"

"See what? Oh, the ship, you mean?"

"No, I mean the dogs walking around like people."

"Oh, that." Spike nodded. He leaned closer and lowered his voice. "Those dogs are Sea Dogs, and that's why they can walk that way. The big one there—" He pointed his muzzle at the largest dog, the one wearing a captain's hat. "—is Captain Rollo, my friend and the head of this whole operation."

Spike led Solo around a boulder, and they stepped carefully down a stretch of trail thick with rocks. Spike spoke softly to Solo. "Sailor dogs have to have 'hands' because they do a lot of jobs to keep their vessel shipshape and running smoothly. Captain Rollo performs a certain ritual, so animals can walk upright and use their front paws pretty much like hands."

"Then he's a magician as well as a sailor?" Solo squeaked. "Are these guys pirates?"

Spike looked down at his front paws for a moment. "Not really, but they'll do what they have to do to protect the open seas that belong to the queen. You'd be surprised at what goes on out in the big world. You need to get off the farm more, my boy!" And with that he gave Solo a nudge. Solo almost stumbled over the last few rocks onto a patch of rough grass.

"I guess," answered Solo. His feet hit the sand. He hated the gritty feeling on his pads, but he swallowed his complaint. Looking back up the path, he sighed. For a moment he wished he was safe in his cozy doghouse, just counting the stars.

A shadow moved up on the rocky pathway, but when Solo blinked and looked again, he saw nothing.

Chapter Four—Solo Becomes a Sea Dog

Spike moved easily in the sand. They drew near the group of dogs around the bonfire. “C’mon, Solo, I’ll introduce you to the captain and his crew.”

Solo sensed his friend’s excitement. “Do ... do you think it’s okay?” Avoiding a grimace, he shuffled along to keep up with Spike. “I mean, are they expecting you...ah, us?”

“Sure, the captain will be expecting me. He made the call.” Spike glanced at Solo, caught his eye, and grinned. “He’ll be glad to see you, too—another sailor.”

“What do you mean?” Solo’s stomach felt as heavy as a bag full of sand. “I’m going to be a ... a ... sailor?”

“He’s recruiting. He’s got a job, an adventure coming up, and he needs more ‘hands.’” Spike saw the fear on Solo’s face.

"Aw, don't worry—I'll bet we'll be back by dawn. Noon at the latest. If you are thinking of your folks, nobody will even notice that you are gone. Or if they do, they'll just think you are exploring in the fields."

"Mittens will notice," Solo fumed.

"So what?" Spike dismissed her as a problem. "Unless she can actually tell your people what you are doing, you have nothing to worry about."

"Oh yeah?" Solo muttered. "If there's some way to get me in trouble, she'll figure it out."

They were getting close but hadn't been spotted yet. "Is that what happened tonight?" Spike asked.

Solo growled under his breath. "Yeah. I was sleeping and she came by and clawed my leg. When I chased her away, I knocked over a table. Abby—that's the mom—made Beth put me in the doghouse for the night." He tilted his head toward the group of dogs. "Oh look, that captain guy has seen us. He's coming over."

"C'mon, Solo. Here we go!" Spike charged off, casting sand into Solo's face.

Captain Rollo strode up on two legs. "There ye be! I heard ye were in these parts—glad to see me ol' pal." He was a huge yellow dog, a German shepherd, Solo thought, though his color suggested golden Lab in his bloodline. The captain grabbed Spike's neck with his front paw and gave him a sort of hug.

Solo tried not to stare at the dog's legs and his front paws waving around like hands. The captain's fur was coarse. Besides wearing a captain's hat, he sported a blue jacket. It had gold buttons with anchors painted on them.

With small, dark eyes, Captain Rollo peered down the length of his narrow nose to look at Solo. "And who's this small guy? Your sidekick?"

Before Solo could protest, Spike answered, "Not a sidekick; he can stand his ground. Solo's a dog who's ready for adventure. Think you might need him too?"

"Aye, sure, sure. 'Tis pirates we're after. Need all the hands I can get. Ye be named Solo?"

Solo felt as if he should salute, but knowing he couldn't actually do that, he merely answered, "Yes." He cleared his throat. "Glad to help … sir."

Captain Rollo clasped Solo at the scruff of his neck, a gesture of acceptance. "Good. Come on and meet the crew, and then I'll tell ye our mission."

The paw on Solo's neck didn't feel exactly like Beth's hand, but it was pretty close. Solo hated to stare, but he did anyway. Dogs walking on two legs and using "hands"—incredible!

Captain Rollo introduced Spike and Solo to a few of the sailors. "Here's me motley crew," the captain boomed. "They came by their names fair 'n square." He pointed to the two closest to them. "These two be Righty and Lefty." Then he pointed to two taller dogs near the fire. "Those tars be Shorty and Stretch."

Solo watched Stretch dip his mug into the kettle and lift it, dripping, to his mouth. He looked away when Stretch yawned, smacked his lips, and scratched his furry belly. As untidy and rough as they all appeared, they walked easily on two legs. Their front paws worked just like hands.

Curiosity made him bolder. "Just how do you manage using your front paws as hands? Walking that way? Is it impossibly hard?" he asked Lefty.

Lefty waved his hand through the air. He leaned closer and rasped, "Nothin' to it. The captain will do his hocus-pocus, and you'll be like us." He had his left paw behind his back.

Solo gulped. "Are you called 'Lefty' for some special reason?"

Lefty leered, his jagged grin reminding Solo of Beth's last Jack-o-lantern. Then Solo saw it, the shining metal of a hook where his left paw should be.

Lefty cut his hook through the air a couple of times. "Aye, you could say so," said Lefty, as he chuckled through that wicked grin of his. "Hey, Righty, show our little pal here your right 'hand', okay?"

Righty obliged, and he was a mirror twin of Lefty. He had a hook where his right paw should be! As Solo stared, Righty hollered, "Hey Shorty, show him why you're called Shorty."

Shorty moved with a limping gait. "Missing part of me leg, lad," he said with a laugh. "I tussled with a shark out there in tropical waters, many years ago. Been called "Shorty" ever since I got me peg leg." He leaned in and Solo cringed as he smelled the sailor's foul breath. "My actual name is Herman, he whispered. "But don't be tellin' these blokes that, or else...." He made a slashing motion across his throat.

Solo backed away from Shorty, then saw Stretch licking his lips, his mug empty. Stretch wiped a paw across his muzzle and belched. "Ah, tasty stuff. Nothing like grog to warm a dog's gizzard." He walked over to Solo.

Stretch had all his limbs, but Solo sensed he was about to find out how that dog got his name.

Stretch rubbed his belly and yawned. "I suppose you want to know why I'm called 'Stretch.'"

Solo nodded.

"Well, see here," Stretch drawled, savoring his moment. "I'm called Stretch because of this!" He bent and thrust his neck at Solo. His neck was mostly bare of fur, and a long black scar roped around it. Solo backed away in horror, and Stretch laughed bitterly. "I was strung up by a band o' pirates. The Cap'n got to me just in time. Saved me by a hair ... or two." His grin rivaled Lefty's. Got me nickname and me scar as mementos."

Solo felt faint. He managed to stand his ground until the other dogs had moved away and began talking among themselves. Then he sagged against the nearest rock. *Oh man. I can't go home maimed! Or worse, be shipped home as a corpse! Or worst of all, never get home! To be eaten alive by a shark or strung up by pirates! Beth would be so sad. I would be so sad. I don't want to do this.* He stole another glance at the path up the cliff. He was wondering if he could get up there without being noticed.

Then he saw her.

Her tail twitching, Mittens perched on a big boulder at the base of the cliff, right where the pathway began. Though he couldn't see her expression, Solo knew she was smirking. She had seen his hesitation, sensed his fear. If he ran back to the farm now, she would razz him for the rest of his life.

He was going to be a Sea Dog.

SL
SOLO

MICK

Chapter Five—Transformation!

Spike came along to rescue Solo from his second thoughts. His fur glowed orangey-red in the firelight. “Hey, ol’ buddy, are you ready to become a Sea Dog? The Captain wants us over by the fire. The transformation ritual will take place there.”

Solo stared up at the full moon hanging like a disk of heavy silver in the dark sky. Would he ever see it after tonight? Would he ever have those slow, lazy evenings in his doghouse again, with nothing much to think about or to worry about? He made up his mind and faced Spike. “Yes, I’m ready. Let’s do it.”

Spike tipped his head to look Solo in the eye. “Good. You realize that you won’t transform successfully if you have any doubts.”

“I said I was ready,” Solo confirmed, but the collar on his neck felt unusually tight. Once he had hands he would loosen it first thing. Or maybe take it off. He smiled in spite of himself. Being collarless might be a blast.

Everyone had gathered at the bonfire. Spike stopped at the largest dog in the group. “Mick, this is Solo, a new recruit.” To Solo, Spike whispered, “Mick is Captain Rollo’s first mate. As fine a Sea Dog as ever lived.”

Mick nodded at Solo instead of saying hello. He bore a few scars on his craggy Mastiff face. A striped, blue and white t-shirt strained against his muscled chest. He pointed to the two dogs beside him. In a deep, rasping voice he said, “Solo. These sorry excuses for sailors be Felbo and Cannonball. Spike says ye’ve met t’other mates.”

Felbo was the roughest-looking standard poodle Solo had ever seen, with a blue-blind eye, mats of curly black hair, and a blue beret that he adjusted with one of his paw-hands. He shrugged indifferently. “ ’allo.”

Cannonball was a fat pug whose build matched his name—he looked like a big black ball walking on two back legs.

Solo gulped so he wouldn’t laugh.

A black belt circled Cannonball’s girth. A sheathed dagger was tucked into it, ready to be grabbed in an instant. At the mention of his name, Cannonball unsheathed the dagger, held it up for all to see, tapped it on his head, then pointed it right at Solo. “You don’t look like much of a sailor.” He snorted. “Landlubber.”

“I lub ... er love the land, but I’m ready to be a sailor. The ocean is like my second home.” If he had been able, he would have crossed fingers behind his back.

Felbo and Cannonball looked at each other and laughed. “We’ll see about that.” Cannonball resheathed his dagger and stepped back.

Mick’s voice rumbled, “Ignore ‘em. They’re all bluster. Gentle as kittens, they be.”

The two Sea Dogs grinned, but their eyes narrowed at this description of themselves. They stepped back into the darkness.

Captain Rollo’s voice boomed over the murmur of the other voices. The noise stopped, except for the occasional crackle or pop of the fire. “Listen up, blokes. We be here tonight on account of an important mission.” He paced back and forth, paw-hands on hips. “One of the queen’s ships has been pirated—looted and destroyed.”

He stopped and shook his head. “The worst of it is ... the worst of it ...” He passed a paw over his eyes. “...is that Princess Esme has been kidnapped!” Gasps and yips rippled through the group gathered in the firelight. Stretch asked, "Does anyone have an idea where they've gone?"

"Just let us at 'em," growled Cannonball. "Me an' Felbo'll save our little princess."

Felbo nodded, winking his bad eye and sneering.

Solo shuddered at the eye and the yellow fangs. He looked up at Spike who hadn't seen Felbo at all. Spike stared intently at the captain.

"Word has it," answered Captain Rollo, "that there be an uncharted island out in the open sea where they be hidin'. I got this information from Queen Esmerelda herself, and directions, too—we can get there in no time with the breeze liftin' our sails."

"Do we know the enemy?" asked Lefty.

"Aye. It's Carbuncle Clyde and his band of scalawags. Rumor 'as it that there's a couple of rogue weiner dogs among 'em." Murmurs sounded through the group. "The scourge of the seas has our pretty miss in his evil clutches." He turned toward Spike and Solo. "Let's transform ye two into sailors and be off."

Solo thought, *Weiner dogs? They've got to be kidding. I know Gizmo, two farms away. He's a weiner dog and he's nuts. Acts real tough but he's a marshmallow.*

Solo brightened. *So this won't be dangerous, after all.*

The captain motioned them to his side. "All right, me lads, be ye ready for this?"

Spike stood in front of the leader of the Sea Dogs. Solo watched him shake himself as if to shed any four-legged limitations. Then he stood still as a statue.

The captain shut his eyes and lifted his long muzzle to the sky. Emitting a mournful howl, he was answered in kind by the rest of his crew. Then, with a snap of his jaws, he cut off the howling.

Eyes still tightly closed, he placed his paws on Spike's shoulders and spoke solemnly and quite formally. "Spirits of the air, land, and sea, we need these two brave hands to get back Queen Esmerelda's daughter." His deep voice carried through the night air. "We must defeat the wicked pirates who have stolen our dear princess and robbed the queen of her most precious gem, her only child."

He turned to Spike. "Spike, me lad, guide the transformation of your body with your mind. Concentrate on your limbs." The captain ran his paws slowly down Spike's forelegs as he recited the magic words:

"As ships upon the sea

Need a handy crew,

Take these legs and use them

As hands one and two."

Solo stared in amazement. Spike was entranced, his head lolling to one side as the captain massaged his front legs. Spike shivered and shook. Sparks seemed to fly from his fur. His toes extended and flexed, each independent of the others. Solo saw his back arching slightly and his fore paws lift off the sand.

"Now for the rest," said Captain Rollo. "Take your paws that are now hands, Spike, and move them up and down your back legs. Careful so's ye don't fall down":

"Front paws now are hands

With this power we beg

As Sea Dogs to stand

And to walk with sea legs."

Spike did it. He took a few hesitant steps on his back legs, walked, then jogged around the fire and the cheering sailors.

"Solo, be ye ready?" the captain asked. Spike gave him a reassuring nod. Solo didn't look at any of the other sailors, though he saw Mick behind Captain Rollo, smiling toothily and nodding as well.

"I am." Solo listened to the same directions and followed them as best he could. As the captain moved his paw-hands up and down Solo's forelegs, chanting the first verse about "hands one and two," Solo felt a burning and trembling in his limbs that he had never before experienced. They tingled and twitched. His toes did their own dance.

His back arched as he listened to the second verse of the spell. His eyes remained closed, and his head drooped down on one side. The same burning and tingling coursed through his back legs as he rubbed them.

He felt himself unfolding into an upright position. Standing on his hind legs, he took a step, then two.

"Come on Solo. Come on, pal." Spike's voice encouraged him.

"I'm doing it!" Solo laughed. "Look Spike! Look Captain! Look Mick! I'm a Sea Dog!"

Chapter Six—Stowaway!

Unbeknownst to the canines circling the fire and yelping, someone watched the ceremony that enabled Spike and Solo to walk upright. Mittens, the small cat, had moved closer to the action by hiding behind a large rock. She made not a sound, even when the dogs she knew wriggled and squirmed and stood upright. When she heard Solo call out that he was a "Sea Dog," her heart beat rapidly. Her whiskers twitched, but she knew she could not even whisper, let alone yowl.

Now the dogs were dancing in a circle. At the captain dog's brusque yip, they went to do different chores. Some plunged jugs into the kettle then stoppered them with corks. Others kicked sand or tossed buckets of sea water to douse the fire. A huge dog in a striped t-shirt waded into the water to get the small boat. A short, round dog and a taller ratty-looking dog helped him drag it to the water's edge. Mittens heard the grumbling growls of those two as they walked back to the others.

The three dogs left the rowboat, and Mittens had an idea. Should she? Would she? She hated water. She had never been as close to the sea as she was right now, but she had to see where they were going. There could be trouble. There could be excitement. She didn't want to miss anything.

No one was looking at the little boat. Seizing her moment, she dashed to the craft and leaped up on its edge. It smelled like wet wood and something else—maybe seaweed, Mittens thought—but it wasn't unpleasant, just unfamiliar and exotic. Underneath one of the seats was a half-rolled tarp.

She saw several dogs approaching, so she darted to the tarp and wriggled far enough in it to be out of sight. Just as she tucked her tail inside, she felt the boat moving. Someone was pushing it back into the water.

"Hey, ho," said Mick. "Ye lads hop inside with the others and I'll row ye out to the ship. Careful with the jugs of grog, there."

Felbo and even the round Cannonball leapt in easily, but it took Spike two tries and Solo three to get inside the boat.

"Not to worry, me boys," Mick said easily. "Ye'll catch on in no time."

The small boat was crowded, but the Sea Dogs settled on the seats for the short ride. Mick jumped into the drifting boat and took up the oars. Solo happened to be sitting on the back seat, and his feet hit the tarp half-wedged underneath him.

"Oooof." A muffled sound carried to his ears.

"What was that? Did you hear anything, Spike?"

Spike turned around to face his friend. "No. What did you hear?"

"I'm not sure. I must have imagined it." Even so, he gently nudged his foot with the tarp. There was no other sound. Then he saw the tip of a striped tail disappear into the coarse blue fabric.

He peered closer, so curious that he hadn't even noticed the boat was afloat and rhythmically being pulled toward the ship. Uh oh, there it was! A bright angry cat's eye glared up at him, and whiskers bristled.

"I could rat you out right now!" he mouthed to Mittens.

The angry eye became a pleading one. *Mittens is right*, Solo thought. *If I say anything, Felbo and Cannonball will kill her. I can't let that happen. Beth would be heartbroken.*

"Oh, all right," he mouthed to the cat's eye. "Just stay far away from me."

The eye winked as if in agreement, then disappeared.

Solo nudged the tarp once more, not quite so gently this time. *If she does anything to make my life miserable, I will rat her out, Beth or no Beth. I'm going to be a good Sea Dog, even if I have to keelhaul a cat.* He wasn't sure what keelhauling meant, but it couldn't be good.

When Solo looked up, the ship loomed close ahead. They were almost in its shadow by now. Solo's heart thumped in his chest. Felbo and Cannonball had three eyes upon him, questioning looks on their scroungy faces. He gulped and looked away.

They pulled up alongside a ladder hanging down from the ship.

"Here we be," boomed Mick. "Welcome aboard the 'Briny Belle.'"

BRINY BELLE
SL

Chapter Seven—On Board

Solo peered up at the rope ladder dangling down to the rowboat, the latest challenge for someone who just had paws turned into hands a few minutes ago. His stomach felt like he was already on the open sea, but they were still in the bay.

He watched as Mick, Stretch, and Cannonball put their paw-hands on the sides of the ladder and hoisted themselves up the rungs. They alternated their back legs as they went. They made it look easy.

Felbo nodded at Spike and Spike exhaled deeply. He followed the sea-worthy dogs up the ladder, stumbling only once. Spike grinned down at Solo from the deck, motioning him to come up too.

"Go ahead, whatever your name eez," drawled Felbo.

"Solo. It's Solo."

"Easy, boy. Don't get all 'uffy." Felbo smirked and blinked his blind eye. "I gotta see this."

Solo flexed his paws that now were like hands. His legs were short. He figured he'd have to pull himself up from rung to rung for his back legs to reach a foothold. He grasped the rope—it felt so funny in his grip. His grip felt funny! But he did it. He pulled himself up and set his back legs on the bottom rung. Then he did it again. Rung by rung, he drew himself all the way up the ladder to the rest of the Sea Dogs. When he tumbled onto the deck, the others shook his paw—even Cannonball.

Mick called down to Felbo, still in the rowboat. "Hey, toss up that tarp before ye go back for the other sailors."

Felbo touched his beret in a mock salute and bent to reach for it.

"Uh-oh," muttered Solo.

"What's that?" asked Mick as they all watched Felbo swinging the tarp back and forth to get momentum.

"Oh, nothing." Solo gritted his teeth as the blue roll hurtled up over the side of the ship and landed with a thump onto the deck. *No 'oof' this time. She's probably knocked cold. Or she's broken her neck.* As irritating as she was, Solo cringed at the thought of Mittens lying lifeless within the tarp. He didn't really want her dead. She was part of Seaview Farm, as much a part of it as he was, really. Beth will be crushed if the cat never came home.

The others turned away to prepare for the sail away. Solo lingered at the tarp, waiting to see movement—a twitch—anything.

He was about to give up. Amazed as he was at the moment of sadness he felt, he soon became annoyed once the blue tarp stirred ever so slightly. It stopped and then the movement started again.

Mittens' head emerged from one end of the roll. She shook it gently, as if dazed, and then did it again. Cautiously one paw came out and then the other. She stretched and pulled the rest of her body out onto the deck. Gingerly, she flexed her limbs as if checking for broken bones. She moved slowly, as if she were slogging in thick mud.

Solo looked at the water and saw the rowboat nearing the ship, the rest of the Sea Dogs aboard. They'd be at this spot in a matter of seconds. How could he get Mittens out of sight? Spike and the rest were now watching the oncoming rowboat, so he had a brief moment to stash the cat.

"Get back in that tarp. Hurry. Quick."

"No way. Couldn't force me to go back in that awful place."

"You've got to—you'll be seen, and I'm telling you, these dogs won't be nice. Some of 'em are as rough as pirates. Make you walk the plank. Keelhaul you. They'll throw you overboard if nothing else."

"You think?" Mittens yawned, still sluggish.

"I *know*. Come on. You have *got* to hide. Omigosh, they've scraped the side of the ship—they're here!"

He scooped Mittens up and she didn't resist. She lay limp in his arms while he staggered here and there, looking for a hiding place. He didn't know anything about ships—what was where or what was what. He spied a door in the wall of the ship's cabin. Pulling it open, no small trick since he still had his hands full of cat, he saw that it was a storage cupboard. It was full of ropes and canvas. He slid Mittens into it and shut the door just as Captain Rollo set foot on the deck.

Chapter Eight—At Sea

"So, how are ye doin', me boy?" Captain Rollo's big voice boomed to Solo as the dog himself approached. Clapping Solo on the back, he continued: "You be gettin' used to your sea legs. Good. Good."

Solo leaned back on the cupboard door, assuming that Mittens had gotten herself out of the way. He didn't hear any complaining or any scratching. He relaxed. "Ah ... yes, sir, that's right, sir."

"Glad to hear it. The rowboat's been stowed, so we can be off. Watch me boy, so's ye can learn how to set sail with the rest of 'em."

The captain then made a commanding bark, and the sailors who had been milling about moved to their positions. Spike had *some* nautical knowledge, but he must have been given a pass this time, too, for he sat on a coil of rope and crossed his hind legs. "Over here, Solo," he called to his friend. "You'll need to stay out of the way."

"Okay." Solo climbed up next to Spike. "Do you know what they are doing?" he asked. They watched as Righty and Lefty worked as one to hoist the mainsail. Stretch worked the jib, and Cannonball climbed up to the crow's nest on a wobbly rope ladder much longer than the one they had used to board the ship. It was easy for Solo to forget that these animals had transformed from four-legged creatures to two. They moved through their tasks with ease.

"More or less." Spike shrugged. "Though it's been a while." He glanced at Solo. "You okay going with us? You sure?"

"Yep. As long as we get back by morning ... or so."

Spike chuckled. "That's the plan, little buddy. We don't want to make our people sick with worry, do we?" The spotted dog checked the claws of one paw. He blew on them and buffed them against his chest.

Solo shook his head. "I suppose not. And Beth, my person, has Mittens to worry about, too."

"Say what?"

"I mean ... what if Mittens wandered off sometime?"

"Who cares?" Spike asked, shrugging. "That would be Mittens' problem, wouldn't it?"

Solo peeked at the storage cupboard where the striped kitten was hiding. "I suppose. That cat is so darn curious, though ... I wouldn't be surprised if she disappeared sooner or later."

"Long as she doesn't show up here. There are some bad dudes here, especially Cannonball and Felbo. Everyone else is all right, but I mean to avoid those two, and I'm not even a cat. I shudder to think what'd happen to a feline."

Solo hurried to change the subject. "What kind of ship is this?" he asked, for he really was clueless about boats and oceans and sailing.

"I dunno. It's a smaller version of the typical sailing ship, I guess. Bigger than a sloop; smaller than a windjammer. Rollo designed it himself." Spike pointed up at the black pug who held an spyglass as he scanned the dark sky. "Too bad the crow's nest isn't big enough for Felbo, too—he and Cannonball wouldn't bug me if they could just stay up there."

Grasping the wheel with one paw, Captain Rollo held up the other to gauge the wind direction. He steered skillfully, adjusting the rudder to turn the ship so the breeze would catch the sails. In a matter of moments, the sails began to billow and fill. Then the ship moved, gliding silently through the water.

I pray I don't get seasick, Solo thought. *I can't be much help if I'm curled up on a gunny sack someplace, retching and moaning.*

As they began to move faster, the dark mounds of land grew smaller until the Sea Dogs at last were on the open sea.

Mick left his spot after securing the boom, and then everyone relaxed and began to move about.

"Are you up to walking on those sea legs?" Spike asked, standing and stretching.

Solo nodded. "I'd better practice in case we hit any rough sea later on." Cautiously, he arose and stretched. He put one foot forward and then the other, willing himself not to grab at anything with his forepaws. "It's okay. I'm doing okay." As they walked along the deck he gained momentum.

"Yer doin' great," Mick said, his grin revealing a couple of gold fangs. "Keep at it. Ye'll be an old salt afore we know it."

Shorty stumped up. "Well, I'll be dad-blasted. Looks like you been doin' that most o' your life."

"Thanks, Shorty," Solo said, putting his hands on his hips. "What is it you do on board?"

"I'm the cook. C'mon along below decks, and I'll show you the galley."

Solo glanced once more at the storage cupboard and said, "Okay." He couldn't be gone too long. He'd have to sneak over and let Mittens out, once he figured out a better place to stow the stowaway. He followed Shorty below decks.

Chapter Nine—Hide and Seasick

Meanwhile, the stowaway herself was having second, third, and fourth thoughts about an adventure at sea. From the first movement, when the boat tilted ever so slightly, Mittens' innards had revolted. She was a pampered land animal, used to roaming about instead of being stuck in a dark and smelly place. She felt sick and half-afraid. The only thing worse right now would be seeing a big, hairy rat—rather, hearing or smelling one—she couldn't *see* anything.

As the ship gained speed, Mittens curled in a ball and moaned. *Oh my, oh myomyomy. What was I thinking? I didn't take all those dumb two-legged dogs seriously! Thought it was all just canine brag and bluster. Where* is *Solo anyway?*

Whenever someone clomped by the storage closet, Mittens held her breath.

The voices she heard were muffled murmurs. She couldn't tell if the voices belonged to Solo or Spike, so she didn't dare make a sound. The wrong dog might be out there.

It seemed like Solo was taking forever. The air grew stuffier with each of her gasping breaths; the dark, if possible, grew even darker. The coiled ropes and the scratchy bits of canvas made her body itch. "Where is that dog?" she hissed.

* * *

Only half-listening as Shorty droned on, Solo, for his part, worried about the little cat. He did realize more than once that he didn't need to. She had made her own trouble and should have to find her way out of it. Then he remembered the people at his home who loved her, so he had no choice but to help her.

Solo was thankful to be spared any sea-sickness so far. He would do whatever he could to avoid that embarrassment. He would need some luck to keep Mittens from being discovered, too. He tried to act interested in Shorty's conversation. The cook talked at length about his galley and his ability to make great grub with limited supplies.

"I thought this was going to be a quick trip," Solo said. "Are we going to need meals?"

"Aye," Shorty said, tapping his peg leg on the floor for emphasis. "The Cap'n likes a hearty supper and a good breakfast—and lunch, maybe. We should have the princess aboard then, and she'll probably be half-starved."

Solo nodded.

"Who knows?" Shorty added. "Might take us longer than a night and a mornin' to accomplish our purpose." He swabbed his counter with a clean cloth. "Plenty o' supplies if we need 'em."

"But, I thought ..."

Shorty winked. "Cap'n always gives the best possible scenario." Seeing Solo's anxious expression, he added, "Don't worry, me lad. Human folks don't follow our timeline so much. Your people shouldn't even notice ye've been gone."

Solo's smile was strained. "Okay."

When Mick came below to chat with Shorty about supplies, Solo escaped to the deck to deal with Mittens.

* * *

Solo approached the storage cupboard. He walked past it, turned, and came back. Over beyond the sails and the rigging, Spike was talking to the Captain as he steered the ship. They wouldn't notice him if he was careful. On the opposite side of the cabin, at the front of the ship, he heard the others' voices raised in song:

"Tis a sailor dog's duty

To take to the sea,

To rescue the princess

And ... (they dragged this word out)

Claim pirates' booty."

Solo could imagine them passing a jug of grog. Which one would be playing the squeezebox? He wondered. Not Righty or Lefty, he thought with a chuckle. Then he heard the nasally French accent and thought, *Felbo. He's the musician. Nasty lout that he is, he can play and sing.*

As the Sea Dogs launched into the next verse, a soft moan interrupted Solo's thoughts. It came from the closet. Solo pulled open the door with care, not sure what he'd see. Two striped legs emerged from the shadows and then Mittens' head. She lay flat on her stomach. Her tongue lolled between her teeth. "Am I dead yet?" she rasped. "What are you—a ghost?" Her eyes were narrow slits. She rolled on her back and clutched her middle. "I think I'm on the way out! It's curtains! Help me! Help me!"

"Look, cat, it's not my fault you decided to sneak onto our ship, and it's sure not my fault that you're sick, so you'd just better look upon me as your rescuing angel."

"Your ship? You an angel? Bleahh!" She continued to rub her stomach and writhe around.

Solo would have been more sympathetic if the darned cat was a little bit grateful for his help. She seemed to assume he should assist her, and that attitude was annoying. "Oh come on," he groused. "It can't be that bad."

"It's that bad!" she hissed.

"Quiet! They'll hear you. And you know what that would mean."

"At least I wouldn't be seasick anymore."

"Oh, come on. I've got to get you out of here—stash you somewhere else." Solo glanced again at the Captain and Spike before he bent to pull the cat up.

Mittens rolled back onto her stomach and dug her claws into the wooden planks. "I refuse to be stashed anywhere. No more dark, smelly places. Just let me lie here on this cool, airy deck."

"What? You're crazy. You'll end up as shark bait." Solo nudged the cat with his foot, stumbling a little as he did so. "Come on."

Spike approached. "Hey, Solo, you ready for the hammock? We'll need to rest before ... what are you doing?"

"Mittens stowed away," Solo confessed, "and now she's really sick." He put his paws under Mittens' arms and pulled her upward. "I have to find a hiding place for her before she's discovered and ruins everything."

Spike rested a paw on his chin. "So that's what you were hinting at earlier. Hmmm. Well, I'm not too surprised. She's a complication, though. Correct-o that she needs to stay hidden." Spike looked at Mittens, limp except for an occasional twitch, and at Solo, who pleaded silently for help. "I've got it!" He slapped his spotted thigh. "To the hammocks. Pronto."

Solo checked all around but saw no one watching as they began to move Mittens out of sight. He forgot to look up, however, or he would have seen Cannonball's spyglass trained right on them.

SL

Chapter Ten—Discovered!

"What do you *mean*, we'll make her our secret weapon?" Solo asked as he and Spike sneaked a listless Mittens down to the sleeping area.

"Simple. If anybody finds out about her, we'll just say she works with us as a top secret agent—a spy."

"The sea air has gotten to you, Spike!" Solo exclaimed.

"Ah, here are the hammocks. Yours and mine are over in this corner." He hoisted Mittens' back legs onto Solo's hammock, but the movement made the cat moan piteously. "I've got an anti-seasick elixir here someplace. I'll give her a dose."

Solo rolled Mittens fully on to the hammock, ignoring her noises. "Where did you get the elixir?"

Spike looked a bit sheepish. "Well, the Captain always has some for me." He patted his midsection. "In case ... you know."

Solo blinked. "Well, it's good you have some, but will it help a cat who's already seasick?"

"It should. Hope so." He lifted his ears and listened, then gestured at Solo. "Here, quickly, step in front of your hammock. Hide her. I hear someone coming."

Spike opened a small pouch stowed by his hammock and pulled out a purple bottle with a stopper in it. "Keep watch. Let me get this into her."

Mittens' mouth lolled open, but at the taste of the dark, strong-smelling liquid, she gagged and hissed. "Ack! Ick!" Her eyes darkened. "You're trying to poison me."

"Shush, cat!" Solo whispered. "Oh hello, Mick. Felbo. What's up?"

Felbo sneered. "Cannonball's up. And he saw everythin', including that heesing striped theeng on the hammock behind you."

"Oh her? A stowaway. Spike and I will deal with her."

"The barnacles you weel. Mick, can we keelhaul that beast? I wanna keelhaul eet."

Mittens sputtered in the hammock, clawing at Spike who held her down. "Easy, cat. Easy."

"Did you hear him? Keelhaul? I don't wanna be keelhauled." Mittens' voice evaporated into gasps and hiccups.

Felbo reached around Solo to grab ahold of Mittens.

Mick held his arm. "Now, hang on. Fair's fair. Let's hear what's going on." When Felbo grimaced, he added, "Mebbe they can explain."

Righty and Lefty had heard the commotion and squeezed down into the cramped sleeping quarters. "What's goin' on? Do we have a stowaway? Did I hear someone say 'keelhaul?'"

Mittens moaned and hiccupped again.

"We'll go above and let the cap'n deal with this," said Mick with the authority of second in command. "Solo, can ye and Spike handle him ... her ... whatever?"

"It's a she and we can," Solo promised.

"We'll be right up," Spike added.

Grumbling and complaining, the others followed Mick up the ladder. Mittens sat up and slashed at the hammock. "Let me outta here."

"The elixir must have taken effect," Spike said. "She doesn't look sick anymore."

Solo grabbed the cat's flailing forelegs. "Will you just hang on? If we work together we might escape walking the plank."

Spike joined in. “What we are going to do, Mittens, is tell them you work as a spy—and that you will help us recover Princess Esme from Carbuncle Clyde and his gang of thugs.”

“Who? What? You’re *nuts*!”

“Did you look at Felbo’s face?” Solo asked her. “He’d like nothing better than to tear you apart. This will be your—our—only chance to save ourselves.”

Mittens struggled less, then stopped and hung her head. “Oh, all right. But I can’t spy!”

“You can and you will,” said Spike. “You’ve spied on us plenty.”

“But that’s different. I know you guys ... you know me. It’s never been ... well ... important ... or dangerous.”

”It is now.” Solo pulled her out of the hammock and set her on the floor. “Come on. You’re hauling yourself up the stairs.”

Up on deck, the night air was fresh and cool. In spite of their predicament, Mittens held her face up and breathed deeply. “Ah. I think I am going to live.”

“Or not,” growled Felbo.

Cannonball had climbed down the rigging and stood beside his pal. “Yeah,” he added, a scowl making his ugly mug even uglier.

Captain Rollo approached Spike, Solo, and Mittens. All the other dogs gathered around them. The captain’s face was solemn. No twinkle lit up his eyes this time. “I see ye hauled a cat on board. Cats ain’t part of our plans. Ever.”

“Wh–what do you want us to do?” Solo asked.

“Get rid of the striped thing. We keep it, they’ll mutiny!” He gestured at the crew who had all gathered there.

Solo glanced at Spike, who swallowed hard, and then at Mittens who held her body very still. Only her whiskers twitched nervously.

“Well. Explain yourselves afore we take care of the problem,” the captain said, pointing at Mittens.

“Sir. Captain ...”began Spike in his most official tone. “It’s like this. Ah ... I know Sea Dogs don’t deal with cats much....”

“Never. Not ever.”

“Well yes, that’s true. But Mittens here...” and he swooped his paw down by the cat and then up again. “... lives on the same farm with Solo. And we know her to be an expert at espionage.”

Mittens tried to puff up her chest and appear seaworthy.

“Hah!” exclaimed the captain. The crew echoed the sentiment.

“I mean it!” Spike exclaimed. “She’s bragged about several top-secret missions she’s been on.”

"Yeah," Solo added, crossing two toes behind his back. "And she got all the way on board here without any of us finding out. She's that good."

Captain Rollo lifted an eyebrow. He pointed angrily at Mittens, then asked "How, by Blackbeard's bones, could she help us tonight?"

Solo forced an idea into his head. "She'll sneak into Clyde's camp and tell us their layout. Nobody'll be looking for a cat, and a cat can sneak around better than anybody."

Mittens' eyes widened and she opened her mouth to protest, but Spike quickly covered it with a paw. "Yeah," he added. She'll be the secret of our plan."

The Sea Dogs murmured among themselves as they considered the idea of a cat helping them. The captain looked thoughtful. Finally, he spoke. "Clyde wouldn't be expecting a cat, by Neptune!"

"I've got a better idea," Felbo said, his craggy smile wicked in the lantern light. "Remember zat tame monkey zat Stretch used to have? He had a leetle red uniform, and it's here someplace. Let's dress ze cat up as a monkey. Then she can be punished but still help out."

Cannonball scurried off to find the monkey clothes.

Mittens shot a paw up, ready to voice her protest, but Solo pulled it down quickly and gave it a warning shake. “Sir, a monkey suit? I don’t think that’s necessary. That would make her too noticeable, wouldn’t it?”

“What you theenk don’t really count,” Felbo warned. ”For zis cat to live, she’s going to have to prove herself. And, she just might save ze landlubbers’ hides also.” He nodded at Spike and Solo.

The other Sea Dogs murmured among themselves. Solo sensed that the murmurs weren’t sympathetic.

“I found it!” Cannonball emerged from the darkness. He held up a cord-trimmed red jacket in one paw and a little red cap in the other.

Spike and Solo caught Mittens just before she slumped to the floor.

SC
FELBO

Chapter Eleven—On with the Mission

"Mick and me'll discuss the plan," Captain Rollo decided. "Put 'er in the brig 'til we decide."

"Een zee monkey clothes?" Felbo asked, grinning.

"Not now," the captain said, and Mittens' heart lifted. "But hang onto 'em," he added as he walked back toward Mick at the wheel. Mittens' heart sank again.

"We got a brig?" Righty asked Lefty.

Lefty shrugged as they wandered down the deck. "Must. Haven't used it for years that I know of. We hardly ever take prisoners, ya know what I'm sayin'?"

Felbo and Cannonball remained after the others had wandered away. They faced Spike, Solo, and Mittens. "Why do you steeck up for zee cat, anyways?" Felbo asked.

"Yeah, cats be dogs' sworn enemies," Cannonball added, waving the monkey clothes in front of a humbled, silent Mittens.

Solo blurted out the answer: "I don't want our family, especially the girl, to be sad because her cat doesn't come home." He didn't care what they thought at this moment. He looked right in Cannonball's eye. Did he detect a flash of some other feeling there before the sneer returned? Sympathy? Envy? Maybe.

"Mon Dieu! Oh zee poor people," Felbo mocked, tapping his chest. Cannonball hastily agreed, chuckling. "To ze brig, to zee brig, to ze brig, brig, brig," they sang as they departed.

"Mittens, you'll have to be jailed for a while." Solo tried to sound nonchalant.

Mittens shrugged. "Don't care."

"I say, old girl, stiff upper lip and all that."

"Nuts," was Mittens' reply to Spike. The three of them looked up as Mick approached.

"I'll take 'er to the brig." It's dry and comfy. I'll leave 'er some water."

Mittens went ahead of Mick without saying a word, though he held a rope in his hands if he needed to grab her.

"It'll work out a'right," he called back to the two dogs. Ye'll see. We'll use her to get back the princess."

"Man, I've never seen Mittens like that," Solo said.

"Didn't seem herself, did she?" Spike stretched and patted his stomach. "Oh, she'll be all right. She's not seasick any more. I'm sure there'll be a hammock in the brig, so she can take a nap."

"At least they didn't keelhaul her," Solo said. "Whatever keelhaul means. And we didn't have to walk the plank."

"Right-o. Say, Shorty was making food. Let's go to the galley and grab some grub."

* * *

With the goings on concerning Mittens, Solo hadn't had time to think about the upcoming adventure. After he and Spike ate, they returned to the deck. The moon hung heavily in the night sky and made a rippled path of silver on the water. The ship glided swiftly along, though Solo had no idea how fast they were actually going. For the moment he felt lazy and content, a direct result of the satisfying meal of fried sausages and potatoes, cornbread, and limeade.

Just now, he didn't anticipate danger, lulled as he was by his full stomach, the motion of the ship, and the beautiful moonlight. He wasn't worrying about the clash with Carbuncle Clyde and his cronies. Mittens' presence on their mission no longer upset him. In fact, he felt a bit sorry for the ornery little cat who wasn't so feisty just now.

He and Spike picked their teeth with slivers of deck wood. They were leaning back against the ship's cabin wall, taking in the night.

"Spike, what does 'keelhaul' mean, anyway? That word keeps popping up in conversations."

"I dunno." Spike murmured, scratching his stomach. "Something bad, old boy. Real Bad. I've never seen a keelhauling myself." He looked up as someone approached. "Here's Stretch. Maybe he can tell us."

"What do ya wanna know?" Stretch grinned and his tongue lolled out the side of his mouth.

"Um ... well, you always hear about 'keelhauling,' and I've used the word myself, speaking as a sailor," Solo explained. "I'd like to know what I'm talking about."

Stretch leaned against the railing. "I've only seen it a couple o'times. It's a bad thing. BAD. Rather wear a red monkey suit than have it happen to me." He winked.

Solo shivered, and Spike sat up to listen.

"A sailor has to have done somethin' really bad. Plannin' a mutiny. Stealing food or plunder. Stabbing a crew mate.

That sorta thing." He gazed out at the dark sea, then resumed his tale. "Both times, the guilty tars had shot one of their own—one over a card game, the other over a female. The cap'n ..."

"Captain Rollo?" Solo asked.

"Yep. He's mellowed over the years. Used to be pretty hard on his crew." Shorty shrugged. "I guess he had no choice with the two he keelhauled. It was terrible. 'Bout finished 'em off."

"What happens at a keelhauling?"

"Well, it's like this. A sailor is tied to a rope that's looped under the ship. He's tossed overboard and pulled under the keel with another rope to the other side of the ship."

Solo drew in his breath. "Can ... can it kill him?"

"Usually does! Shorty exclaimed. "The two I saw survived, but barely. They was scratched up terrible from barnacles and such on the hull. Spit up salt water for days. When we hit land, they swore off sailing forever more. They moved to the desert someplace—prospectin' for gold now. Don't ever want to be reminded of the sea again."

Well, I won't be tossing that word around anymore, Solo mused. *Don't want to be giving anyone ideas.*

"We'd better get some shut-eye," Spike said. "Come on, Solo, let's go to our hammocks."

"All right," Solo said, still thoughtful. Without too much trouble, he went down the narrow steps and climbed into his swinging bed. He was asleep in a moment.

* * *

It was still dark when they heard the cry. One by one, the sleepy dogs climbed from their quarters to the main deck. They saw Cannonball pointing and turned their gazes in that direction.

"Land ho!" Cannonball's voice called from the crow's nest.

"Look." Shorty pointed toward the dark mass at their port side.

Solo and Spike scrambled to the railing. By the light of the moon, they could see the hilly island. A large ship, larger than the Briny Belle, lay anchored in the sheltered cove. Pinpricks of light were visible on shore.

"Bonfires. We're looking at Carbuncle Clyde's island hideaway," Spike said softly.

"Can't they see us?" Solo whispered.

"Not yet, but we'd best not move any closer," Shorty said. "Clyde's a bad 'un, and so are his crew. He's on the scent of a fortune. Ransom. As if the plunder weren't enough. He'll stop at nothing. We've got to surprise 'em or we don't have a chance."

And Mittens is our surprise? thought Solo. *We're sunk. We're harpooned. We're fishbait.*

Chapter Twelve—Plans Take Shape

Solo was fully alert now. Spike stood next to him, and Solo could feel the excitement tensing the other dog's body. Stretch motioned to Righty and Lefty who were approaching. Mick came up behind them. Whispers traveled through this cluster of Sea Dogs on the deck. Everybody who wasn't at a post had gathered. Then, silently, like a bat on the wing, Cannonball swung down the rope ladder and moved past the group.

"Where's he off to?" Solo asked.

"SHHHH!" hissed Mick. Then he whispered, "Cannonball and Felbo are goin' ashore to assess the situation."

"Yeah," added Shorty. "They're the sneakiest dogs we got. When they get back, the Cap'n will know what to do." He pointed to the water. "Looky there."

The rowboat was being lowered to the water. The well-oiled pulleys guiding the ropes didn't make a squeak or a creak. Solo felt like he was watching a scene on the TV with the sound off. Without so much as a rippling noise, Cannonball and Felbo dipped oars into the water and slid away into the darkness. Solo caught the gleam of daggers clenched in their jaws. Leather belts were slung around their middle with pistols wedged in them. He gulped. Armed to the teeth, they were.

Excitement lifted the hackles of the Sea Dogs. Whispered conversations buzzed as they paced back and forth, wondering what the news would be. Solo's emotions shot from excitement to fear to dread while the moments ticked away. He had no idea what was going to happen next.

The moon rose higher in the sky and had just begun its downward path toward the horizon when they all heard a soft scrape along the hull.

"They're back!" exclaimed Spike in as quiet a voice as he could manage. "Now we'll know what we have to do." He and Solo looked at the others.

Mick motioned to them, indicating that a meeting was going to start. Righty and Lefty remained on deck, while everyone else gathered in Captain Rollo's cabin to hear the plan.

The cabin was crowded, but at least they could speak above a whisper here. Stretch pulled Spike and Solo over in front of him so they could see and hear everything.

Captain Rollo had taken off his jacket and put on a black turtleneck and a black cap. His yellow fur stuck out around his ears and his waist. From a bin, Mick fished out similar items and tossed them to the others. Everyone going ashore would be clad in black clothing, whether or not they were already black.

Except, maybe for Mittens. Solo saw the little red monkey suit lying on the captain's desk. He shook his head, relieved that he wore a black turtleneck sweater and cap.

The captain's expression was grim. "All right, mates. This won't be easy, but we know what to do." He nodded at Cannonball and Felbo, who puffed out their chests with importance. Everyone jumped when the captain slammed his fist on his desk: "We will succeed —or Queen Esmerelda's line is doomed."

Solo figured the time wasn't right to ask about dog royalty. Before tonight, he didn't know anything about Sea Dogs, let alone a kingdom where dogs ruled—other than in the best human homes, he thought. He'd ask somebody later—after the mission was completed.

Captain Rollo continued: “Clyde, that scalawag—he’s got three Princess Esmes tied up around his camp.”

“Three? What do ya mean?” Stretch asked, voicing what everyone wanted to know.

“Decoys. The first thing we do is find out which one is the real Esme. Then we’ll be able to whisk her out of there.” The captain looked solemn.

“How well are they guarded?” Mick wondered.

“Felbo ... you tell ‘em,” said the captain.

Felbo, pleased to have all eyes on him, cocked his red beret and let his one-eyed gaze travel past everyone in the room. He rapped the table once, twice, three times, flourishing his paw each time for dramatic effect. “Three guards per preencezz.” Gasps rippled through the group. “And they got plenty of other crew, too, though zee guards looked like they would rather be partying.”

Solo spoke up. “Some are weiner dogs, right? How hard can it be to overtake a pack of hot dogs with legs?”

The Sea Dogs howled with laughter. Felbo doubled over, holding his stomach. When he could talk again, he gasped, “They ain’t yer common, domestic wiener dogs—they’re HUGE!”

"And there ain't a dog more vicious than a rogue, oversized wiener dog!" Mick added. "Stay away from 'em." He scowled at the others. "Ain't no laughin' matter."

Spike and Solo looked at each other. Spike shrugged his shoulders.

Cannonball got back to the business at hand. "The beach is curved. Palm trees line the grassy areas where the sand ends. Clyde and his crew are on the east side—like so." He moved a gyroscope, an ink bottle, and a cigar box around the captain's desk to illustrate the main areas of the pirates' camp.

He took three of the captain's quill pens from their stand and placed them on the west side of the camp to show where the one real and two fake princesses were held.

Felbo nodded his agreement. "Yeah, we thought once we found out zee true preencezz, we'd create a diversion on zee east side. Then the others move in and get her."

"Right, mates," agreed Captain Rollo, and the others nodded their heads.

Cannonball grinned at Felbo. Then Felbo continued: "It's like this. Zee real Esme's a white poodle, right?" He kissed his paw then flung it outward. He put his beret over his heart, and his eyes drifted half-shut. "Everyone knows that. A beauty, too—zee pride of my heritage—I could imagine her at zee tower Eiffel, eating a truffle ..."

"Enough of your fancy talk," said Stretch. "How we goin' to get past all the pirates and rescue the real princess, not a bogus one?"

Felbo shrugged and tilted his head at the captain. "Zee true preencezz? Will she not be obvious?" He set the beret back on his head.

The captain shook his head. "Maybe—maybe not. They might be dirty, but Esme might be too, after the kidnapping.

"All three'll be white poodles. But, the true princess has a birthmark, shaped like a small dragonfly, just so ..." and Captain Rollo pointed to a spot under his right arm.

A chuckle or two was heard among the dogs until the captain stared them all into silence.

Felbo blinked his blind eye and readjusted his beret.

The captain spoke again. "We need a small dog to sneak past the guards without being caught ... a friend of the cat who's goin' along too." All eyes turned to Solo.

"What?" Solo exclaimed.

Spike put a paw on Solo's back to steady him.

"Ye up for the job, Solo?" their leader asked.

All eyes were on him. What else could he do? Felbo and Cannonball smirked. They expected him to say no. Hoped he'd say no. Standing upright, Solo answered the captain. "Yes, sir. When do we start, sir?"

"I'd like to go along with them as backup, if you please, sir," said Spike. "Since we came together." Solo sagged with relief against his friend's arm.

"Ye'll be going ashore, Spike," said Captain Rollo, "but I have other plans for ye. Most of us will be close by as backup, anyhow. We'll have to act quickly. Now this is how it's going to work."

"Want me to go get the prisoner?" Cannonball waved the red monkey suit. "She should know what the plan is, too."

"Aye. Get the cat," said the captain. "Leave the suit here, Cannonball. Don't be so keen on dressin' the cat, okay?"

Captain Rollo turned to the others in the room. "All right, men. The cat and Solo will sneak into Carbuncle Clyde's camp and get past the guards. Once they get the true princess, they'll bring her to us. Meanwhile, some of us will rile up the pirates. Once we get the princess on board, we'll sail before Clyde knows what happened."

"We are going to do this without being seen, I hope," Solo said.

"Aye. Sure. But we'll need a fallback plan in case ye are discovered."

All turned toward the doorway in time to see Cannonball dragging Mittens into the cabin. Mittens had her claws dug into the floor, and her face was a mask of anger.

Oh no! thought Solo, his heart thudding in his chest like a hasty drumbeat.

SL
CAPTAIN ROLLO

Chapter Thirteen—Tactical Plans

Spike nudged Solo and whispered, "Look at her! She's not going to cooperate at all."

Solo felt sick. "She's going to have to. I'm not going to risk my life on my own." He nodded towards Mittens. "We'll have to talk to her."

Spike smiled. "Maybe we won't have to. Look, Captain Rollo's taking her out on the deck. Maybe he'll talk some sense into her."

"If only," Solo said, rubbing his temples. "Wow, he took the red monkey suit out there with them. She's going to be sorry she didn't come willingly."

The captain shut the door firmly as he left. Now all the Sea Dogs turned to one another, discussing the problems involved in their quest for the Princess Esme.

Many glances strayed toward the door, especially when they heard a thump or a scrape. Solo would have worried a bit if he hadn't remembered that the cat's attitude had caused her problems. "As long as it's not a keelhauling," he murmured aloud.

"Keelhauling!" Felbo echoed in a much louder tone. "Excellent for zee nasty little beezt."

Solo and Spike didn't say anything.

Soon the door opened. Captain Rollo, his hair sticking out more than ever, stepped back into the cabin. Behind him came Mittens, also walking on two legs! She had transformed. Her ears were tucked under the little red cap on her head. An elastic band under her chin held it snug. The red military jacket fit her body pretty well. All the brass buttons but the bottom two were fastened. Except for the stripes on her fur and the shortness of her tail, she could pass for a monkey—or would at a distance, anyway.

Her expression was unreadable. Even when the dogs erupted into loud guffaws and slapped their thighs and pointed, Mittens said nothing. She stood right up on the desk as if she wore a red monkey suit and walked on her back legs every day.

When the Sea Dogs realized that they couldn't make the cat miserable, the laughter stopped. Cannonball and Felbo's loud taunts shrank as fast as popped balloons.

Solo didn't know what to think, and from the confusion on Spike's face, he didn't know either. Solo did have a question, though. "Captain Rollo, I thought someone had to be convinced he or she wanted to walk on two legs before the transition would work. How did you get Mittens to do it?"

"Desperate times call for desperate actions," he said plainly. "I told her she had to do it, and she did, by Neptune!"

Mittens twirled her whiskers with her paws that worked like hands now, and continued to appear relaxed and comfortable. She nodded slowly.

"Well, I'll be ..." muttered Solo.

"Now that everybody's listening," continued the captain, "Here's what's goin' to happen. Time's a wasting.

"The monkey-cat will sneak into camp with her 'owner,' Solo. Find out which Esme's real. Win her trust to check the birthmark. Persuade her they be there to save her."

"And we do this how?" asked Solo.

"I trust ye to figure it out," responded Cap'n Rollo.

"So why the monkey costume?" asked Righty who couldn't suppress a smirk. Righty and Lefty had seen the captain's tussle with the cat, so they joined the others in the cabin.

"Alas and alack, just a little more cover—a monkey on the island's more believable than a cat. And especially to entertain pirates."

"Coming from where?" asked Spike.

Felbo answered, "There must be a couple of veellages on zee island. From one of 'em, just guessing."

"Could that possibly work? What entertainment are you talking about?" Solo wondered.

Captain Rollo explained. "Music. You'll have the concertina, Felbo's squeezebox, with ye, and the monkey will dance."

"What! I don't have a clue about music! Nothing! Nada! Mittens, help me out here."

Mittens' eye color deepened to gold and her pupils narrowed into slits, but she did not speak.

"Hey! I don't want heem wrecking zee instrument!" Felbo complained. "Was me mama's."

Mittens remained unruffled. She brushed some imaginary lint off the epaulet on her shoulder.

The captain tried to reassure Solo. "Not to worry. If you be careful, you won't be needin' to play anything." He faced the annoyed black poodle. "Felbo, me lad, it'll just be a prop. For the princess' sake."

"Yeah, well, he'd better take care of eet, or else..."Felbo shook a fist at Solo.

Spike stepped in. “Stop threatening my friend, here.” To Solo he said, “You and Mittens will succeed. You have to.”

“What about you, Spike? Why can’t you help me?”

“Well, I … ah, the Captain said he has a separate plan for me—I have something else to do.”

Solo said, “Then why can’t somebody experienced like Felbo do it?”

“The black poodle’s too big,” answered Captain Rollo. “We need a monkey and dog team who look nothin’ like sailors.” The captain leaned in to whisper in Solo’s ear, “’Sides, he might scare the princess—look at him.”

Solo gulped. “Yeah, I guess you’re right.”

Mittens sat down on the desk, her back feet dangling off the edge. She eyed the motley group of dogs with disdain but continued her silence.

“The rest of us will wait until we get the signal. Then we’ll create a commotion while Mick and Spike grab the princess.”

“How?” murmured the crew.

Captain Rollo paused for effect. Then he exclaimed, “Fireworks! I’ve saved up a few boxes of firecrackers, flares, and bottle rockets. Perfect use for ‘em.”

Righty rubbed his hand against Lefty’s hand. “Argggh. This’ll be good. They’ll think a million guys are firin' on 'em. Argggh!"

"Aye, they'll run for the hills and we'll get our princess." The captain paced back and forth, gesturing. "Shorty and Stretch'll stay aboard. Soon's we make it back, we'll set sail. We'll be heroes to Queen Esmerelda and the princess—save the royal day."

The captain rubbed his shoulder. "I feel it in me old sea-farin' bones. It'll go off without a hitch."

Everybody cheered. Someone yelled, "Let's go." Someone else crowed, "Hooray for the princess!" Dressed in their black clothes, the Sea Dogs streamed from the cabin to get ready for the rescue operation.

Solo knew it was really going to happen when a scowling Felbo thrust his concertina into his paws. "Guard zis with your life you leetle ..." He swiped his eye with an angry gesture. "Eet belonged to my mama."

CANNON BALL

Chapter Fourteen—The Mission Begins

Two rowboats were lowered carefully into the dark water. The Sea Dogs watched the slight bob each made as it touched the surface and floated there.

Solo raised his eyes to the huge moon, now cream-colored, that hung just a touch lower in the sky than it had when he had looked at it last. “How long ‘til morning?” he whispered to Spike. He felt an intense pang of homesickness and couldn’t wish it away. “I want to get home before Beth thinks I am lost—or worse.”

“Time out here goes slow—much slower than human time,” Spike answered. He moistened a paw from a puddle on the deck and held it up. “Slight breeze from the west. Hope it picks up when we’re ready to go.” He turned back to Solo. “Don’t worry. We have time to serve Queen Esmerelda and get back to our homes. It'll turn out fine—you'll see. No human will be the wiser. They think we go on midnight jaunts right in our neighborhood."

"Even though I've never done that in my life," Solo murmured.

Spike pointed at the moon. "See, it's barely moved though we've been in that cabin for a long time."

Solo sighed. "I guess you're right. We better get to it. What are you going to be doing, Spike?"

"I'll tell you later, pal. It's top secret for now—"

Mick brought Mittens over to them. He handed her off, making sure that Solo and Spike each had an arm on her. "I've got to man the second boat. The cat's in your charge 'til further notice."

Mick hurried off, leaving them with a dressed-up, two legged cat—and as it turned out, an extremely angry dressed-up, two-legged cat.

"I have never—I mean never—been so humiliated in my life! I'm so glad my mother is not alive to see this!" Mittens stomped her feet and tried to shake off their hands. "Better to end up road kill than to see your favorite child go through this."

"Well, swash my buckle," chuckled Spike. "The Mittens we know and love is back."

"Look, you're stuck in the red band uniform, and you know you have to cooperate. It's the only way we'll get to go back home," Solo grumbled. He had just about had it with her.

"I know, I know," said Mittens. Her feet stopped their angry dance. "I'll cooperate. That, or walk the plank."

"Is that what the captain threatened?" Solo asked.

"That, among other things," Mittens answered.

"Captain Rollo can be very persuasive," said Spike, smiling.

The little cat sneered at the dogs. "I'll do this to save some dumb dog princess. But you are going to owe me—big time."

"I'm not going to owe you anything, Mittens. You will owe me for saving your striped hide."

Mittens changed the subject. "Let's get going. See, the others are getting into the boats. Hurry, or we'll get stuck sitting next to that one-eyed poodle and that fat pug. Hurry!"

One after the other, they swung down the ladder into the second boat. Using paws as hands came easily to Mittens. She was the fastest one.

Mick and Righty were there already. Mick and Spike set the oars in the water, and they moved off. Their boat had the boxes of fireworks. The first boat held the captain, Felbo, Cannonball, and Lefty.

"Maybe Righty and Lefty should have stayed behind and the other two have come," whispered Solo. "After all ..." He touched his paw.

"They're as good as any two-handed Sea Dogs," Mick responded. "In fact, they find ways to use their hooks that make them even better than the rest of us. Ye'll see."

They steered the rowboats into the shadows of craggy rocks fringing the beach on the west side. Earlier, the scouts had discovered a small cove where the rescue party could stash their gear close by but hidden from view. Mick, Righty, and Solo unloaded a small wheeled cart as Spike secured the rowboat. Then the three of them piled the boxes of fireworks on the cart while Mittens leaned against a rock and cleaned her tail.

Cannonball scrambled up the rocks and peered through his spyglass to get their exact bearings and to see what was what. The entire rescue party then gathered around the cart to hear any last-minute instructions.

"Looks good," Cannonball reported after he came back to the group. "The princess' guards have moved down the beach. They're drinking grog and swapping stories, though they look back pretty often. Each princess is tied to a different log, and there's a fire in the center of the area. They're basically alone, so we need to act now."

"I sure can't tell from here which one might be the real Esme." The black pug nudged Mittens so hard that she lurched forward. "Ol' sharp-eyed monkey here will figure that out right enough."

The Sea Dogs chuckled. Captain Rollo drew Solo and Mittens aside. "Ye know what to do? Everything depends on the two of ye."

"Uh, Sir, any specific ideas how to check out the birthmark?" Solo asked. "I mean, what if a princess starts barking or something?"

The captain lifted a chain from his neck and held it out to solo. A gleaming gold coin dangled from it. "The true princess will ken this as mine," he said. "If Esme can see it—she'll show her mark."

Mittens spoke. "He can't wear that thing—it'll drag on the ground and trip him up!"

"All right, cat, you figure out how to take it." The captain held it out to her.

"Got it," Mittens said. She plucked the necklace out of Captain Rollo's hand and put it under her red cap. "Safe and sound,

Sir." To Solo she said, "Let's go and get this over with."

"How will we signal to you that we've found the true princess?" Solo asked Captain Rollo.

"As we move the cart of fireworks into position, I'll have Cannonball keep his eye trained on you two. When you see the dragonfly birthmark, swing the medallion around over yer head. Then once the three of ye get movin', we set off the firecrackers and the other noisy stuff."

"I always hated fireworks," muttered Mittens to Solo. "Now I know why."

PRINCESS
ESME
LADY
MIMI

Chapter Fifteen—Darling Esme, Esme, and Esme?

"Solo, have you got a plan?" Mittens hissed at him once they had moved away from the others. "We better have something in mind, or else ..."

Solo waited to answer until the last whispered "good lucks" and "go-get'ems" had carried over the air from the others. Wistfully, he peered back at the Sea Dogs. They were getting ready to push and bump the fireworks-laden cart over the soft, shifting sand. Spike saw him and gave him a hearty wave.

"No, I don't really have a plan. Not yet."

"Oh, no!" Mittens gasped. "This is awful! We're going to be dead meat, probably roasted and served on a stick." They moved around the rocky outcropping that had hid their little band from the pirates' view. Mittens stomped through the sand, brushing aside the blades of rough sea grass. "Ouch! This stuff is sharp! Oh, what a nightmare." She looked skyward. "Wake me up, Mama. Pinch me and tell me I'm dreaming."

"Move a little closer," Solo said. "I can't pinch too well, but I can nip."

"Ooh, the captain's necklace is driving me crazy," whispered Mittens. "Maybe I'm allergic to gold." She pulled it out from under her cap and held it out to Solo. "You take it."

"I've already got this concertina of Felbo's to carry." Mittens glared at him. "Oh, all right," he conceded, "I'll loop it around the handle and carry it that way."

Mittens rubbed her head then replaced the cap. "That's better. Now I can think. Three princesses, they said, right? And the real Esme's got that nasty birthmark. Yuck."

"Let's stop here and talk this through," Solo said. They had reached the shelter of a sand dune. "We're getting close to their camp, so we have to be as quiet as possible. If we can get near enough to see the captives' fur, can't we tell real from fake?"

"Great idea, as long as they didn't use other white poodles as their decoys."

"You're right, Mittens, for once. I'm sure that's just what they did." Solo thought some more. “We also don’t know if the fake princesses are part of Clyde’s gang or other captives. Cannonball said they’re gagged but we don’t want ‘em yelling out if we remove the gags.”

Mittens pointed to the concertina. “Well, you have that, and I’m in this monkey suit, so we’re s’posed to act like we’re musicians. That will give us a reason to be in camp.”

“As long as I’m not expected to play and you dance!” Solo hesitated for a moment. He couldn’t help himself. He chuckled ... and chuckled again.

“What a picture that would be!” yelped Mittens. She stopped. Then she chuckled too. “It is pretty crazy when you think about it.” She fell to the sand and rolled around in a fit of muffled laughter. “Who would have thought ...” she giggled some more ... “two animals from Seaview Farm would end up in a mess like this.”

Solo recovered first. “Dust yourself off. We can laugh as loud as we want, later. Let’s get going.”

“Okay,” agreed Mittens, wiping tears from her eyes. “I needed that.” She got up and shook sand off herself. “Here, let’s climb to the top of this dune, hide behind that grass up there, and get the lay of the land.”

Solo agreed. The sand was thick. They struggled up to the vantage point. The long grass waved in the night breeze, and the rough blades rasped as they rubbed against each other.

Solo whispered. “Okay. There’s the fire with the three captives circled around it.” He pointed. “See? And further down the beach there? Most of the motley crew are singing and telling yarns.”

“They are all grogged up, looks like,” Mittens added. “Good, that’ll make them careless and clumsy.”

“And do you see under those palm trees at the edge of the sandy grass? Across the way?” Solo pointed again. “That’s the rest of the pirate camp. In there somewhere is Carbuncle Clyde himself, scourge of the seas.”

Mittens made a gagging motion. “Hope we don’t encounter that creep.”

They turned their gazes back to the princesses. “Which one do you think is our real Esme?” Solo asked Mittens. “They all look about the same from here.”

“Well, one’s nodding her head like she’s almost asleep. If that’s the real one, she’s pretty relaxed. The one closest to us looks nervous; she keeps looking at the pirates. Maybe she’s the true princess.”

“Yeah,” agreed Solo. “But the third one, the farthest away, is just sitting there, staring at the fire. From here, her fur looks the nicest, so maybe she’s the captain’s little darling, Esme.”

"Let's sneak over to her first," suggested Mittens. "We can work our way back to the others, but I'm hoping we don't have to." She looked over her shoulder. "Those pals of yours said they'd have us covered, correct?"

"Yeah."

"Well, I don't hear or see them," the cat said. "Either they're very good at laying low or we're going to have to fend for ourselves."

Solo didn't want to think about that. "They'll be there. Cannonball's watching us right now, waiting for the signal. I'd stake my sea legs on that."

"Whatever," Mittens retorted. "Well, do I go first or do we go together?"

"I say we go together but sneak behind stuff until we get to the far princess. Then we'll have to be careful. We don't want to surprise her and make her bark through her gag." Solo hesitated. "I just don't know how they'll react to us."

"Come on. You know they see striped monkeys in red suits and scruffy squeezebox players all the time." Mittens took a deep breath. "Let's do it. Once we get to number one, I'll get her attention and you can check out her armpit for the dragonfly birthmark." Mittens shuddered. "Oh, ick."

She started first, army-crawling through the grit until she made it to another clump of tall grass in the sand. She motioned for Solo to follow.

He did, ignoring the scratchy feel of the sand as it came through his turtleneck and touched his skin. The wool cap itched on his head. The concertina thumped a little as he dragged it along, but the wind in the grass kept the sound from carrying. *If it gets damaged, oh well,* he thought. *I'll worry about Felbo later.* Once he got to Mittens, he exhaled with relief.

They kept moving that way, stealthily crawling from one hillock or clump of grass to the next, until they were finally close enough to make out the crackle of the fire. They could also hear the voices of the reveling pirate dogs, fading and swelling with the gusts of wind.

As long as they keep singing, Solo thought, *we haven't been seen.*

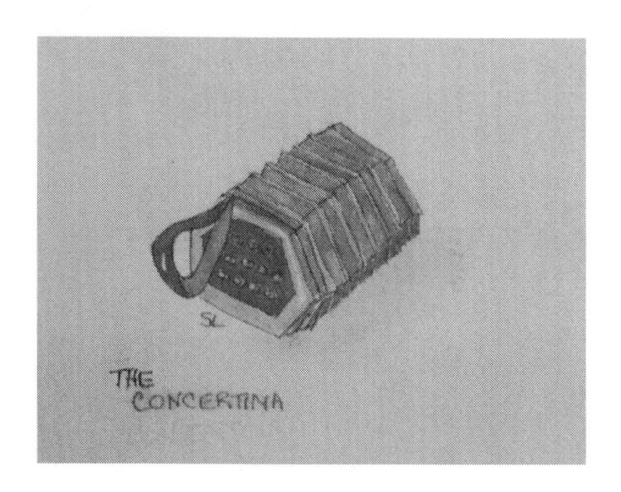
THE
CONCERTINA

Chapter Sixteen—The Rescue!

At last, Mittens and Solo were behind the log of the farthest princess. They hoped she was the true one. She hadn't seen them. She sat as still as ever, as if entranced by the bonfire's bright flames and glowing embers.

She has a fine head, Solo realized. It looks very regal. A soiled and torn ribbon dangled from each ear. Mittens pointed to them and nodded. Maybe the ribbons were evidence that this was the princess, the authentic Esme.

Mittens peered over the log and then nudged him. "Look here!" she mouthed, then pointed at the princess's rope bindings. There was a short rope between her front paws, and a longer one leading from that to the larger rope around her waist.

Mittens nodded, and Solo figured out what she was thinking. The princess's arms would be able to move enough to show her underarms. "You won't have to bother her by pulling on a rope or anything," Mittens added.

Solo drew his paw across his forehead in the universal sign of relief. "Unfortunately," he whispered, "her hind feet are bound, so untying them will slow us down."

"As if this wasn't going to be hard enough, anyway," Mittens mouthed. She stood up straight, wet her whiskers and smoothed them back, and curled her tail into as monkey-like a curve as she could. "Here goes."

Still peeking over the log, Solo watched in amazement as the cat-turned-monkey strutted out into the firelight. If he didn't know better, he'd almost think she was a monkey, although a rather odd-shaped, odd-colored one. Mittens jumped. She frisked. And when she jabbered, she caught the attention of this princess. So far the other two hadn't noticed a thing.

Solo, with his squeezebox, had moved to the end of the log and peered around it. The princess's eyes widened even more when she saw him, too. She struggled to say something, but the gag was too tight. This Princess Esme, with the raggedy ribbons, worked her forepaws and strained against her bindings.

Did she want their help? Or was she trying to alert the crew of pirate dogs? Right armpit. Right armpit. Solo remembered where the birthmark was located. He walked out on his two legs, holding the concertina as if he was going to play it. He hoped it was right-side up. He'd never looked at the thing closely, and now wasn't the time.

He fiddled with the instrument, stalling for a moment or two. He'd have to get close to this poodle—but how would he approach this frightened dog and not alarm her?

Mittens picked up a palm frond and sashayed over to this Esme, whose eyes were still wide with what? Shock? Alarm? Fear? Whatever it was, they had to get her to lift up her arms.

Mittens waved the palm frond in front of the poodle's eyes, and the dog lifted her arms to avoid her face being tickled. Dropping the concertina in the sand, Solo moved in closer. The firelight glowed brightly. He invaded the captive's space and prayed he wouldn't get smacked. He could see … he could see … NOTHING!

"Mittens! Let's go! Next princess!" Mittens turned and cavorted with the palm frond as if entranced. Had she forgotten what they were doing? Solo nudged her. She turned with a scowl but dropped it when he hissed, “NO birthmark! Next dog!”

Mittens grabbed the concertina, and thrust it into Solo’s paws. They hurried toward the next Princess Esme. Behind them they heard the grunts of the first captive as she tried to work herself free. She was obviously the pirates’ alarm system while they weren’t around.

The dog they approached looked directly at them. Is this one friend or foe? Solo wondered. Now we have a one in two chance of her being a friend, at least. They acted calm as they drew closer and closer, but really they were wild with excitement and fear.

The sand wasn’t any easier to get through, no matter the urgency they felt. Solo’s feet dragged like lead weights even as he hurried. When he peered in the direction of the pirate camp, he saw that all was quiet there. So far, so good. And further down the beach, the guards still partied and caroused. He was amazed. Then he remembered poodle number one, trying to get loose. She was a decoy, but also a lookout.

“Okay, Solo, how do we check this one out?” asked Mittens, panting.

“Same way, but we don’t have time for any monkey business first.”

"Haw, haw, HAW!" sneered Mittens. "I'm cracking up."

Solo snapped, "Come on, you doofus—we have to MOVE!" He nudged her. "Grab another palm frond and get tickling."

"Okay, okay." Mittens did so. Solo moved close to this Princess Esme, daintier than the first one and dirtier, too. Her gag was also tight, but above the scruffy bandana he beheld the most beautiful eyes he had ever seen.

Solo was sure one dark eye winked at him. His breath slipped away. He felt faint as he gazed into the smoky depths of this dog's eyes. She had to be the princess. There was a gentleness, a beauty about her ...

It was Mittens' turn to do some nudging. "Wake up, doofus yourself," she said aloud. "Check for the dragonfly."

"Oh, yeah." Before Solo moved closer to this Esme, he peered back at the impostor they had left behind. She had almost worked her paws free! They didn't have much time. This one had better be the princess.

Solo avoided this captive's eyes as he moved to her right side. She sensed what he was doing and lifted her arm as best she could—and there was the wee dragonfly! Here was Princess Esme!

Solo remembered the medallion. He'd forgotten all about the Captain's coin that was to show the princess who they were. And she had trusted them anyway! He'd show it to her now before he signaled the rescuers. He grabbed the squeezebox—but the medallion was gone! Wrapped so carelessly around the handle, it must have worked loose somewhere in the vast expanse of sand.

Just then, an earsplitting howl arose from the first "princess." Her gag was off, and she was alarming the pirates as she worked to untie her hind feet.

"We have to go! Now!" Mittens fussed with the ropes that bound the real princess' paws. "C'mon, Solo. Send the signal. Let 'em know we've got her."

"I ... I don't have the medallion!" he hissed. "That's how I was to alert them." He glanced at the sand around them, but it was nowhere to be seen.

"Well, think of something!" exclaimed Mittens. "I'm working on these knots. You get her gag off."

Solo removed the princess' gag and waved it around over his head the way he was supposed to have swung the medallion. He flapped his arms a few times for good measure—maybe they'd think of the dragonfly that way. Solo prayed that Cannonball had seen and understood what was happening

Princess Esme coughed and cleared her throat but didn't speak.

"We're friends of Captain Rollo," Solo whispered. "How stiff are you? Will you be able to run?"

The princess nodded and struggled with her bindings. Mittens had freed her hands and they both worked on her back legs.

The three of them stopped for just a moment as they heard the pirates' howls and yelps carry up the beach. The alarm had been heard. It was only a matter of seconds now before Clyde's men would be upon them.

The princess was hoarse when she spoke: "Thanks be you've come." After rubbing her wrists, she pointed to the third bound poodle, the one who had been so nervous and who was panicking now. "We're not leaving without Lady Mimi," Esme rasped. "She's under my protection."

"Dog's honor be blasted!" yelled Mittens. "C'mon Princess Esme, we've got to go—NOW!"

Solo gulped. He could feel Esme's dark eyes upon him. "As you say, Your Majesty. I'll go untie Lady Mimi." Princess Esme's bindings were off. "Mittens, start off with the princess, and I'll get her lady friend."

"You're crazy, you know that?" Mittens retorted. She turned to Esme. "C'mon Princess, let's get out of here."

MICK

Chapter Seventeen—A Noisy Escape

Solo mustered his courage and dashed headlong into danger. Mittens and Princess Esme hurried as fast as they could into the darkness beyond the firelight. None of them noticed the activity in the treetops above their heads.

Cannonball had understood Solo's frantic movements when he had discovered the true Esme. The Sea Dogs had been busy since that moment. Had Solo and the rest of his party looked up into the palm trees, they would have been comforted at the sight of Lefty and Righty climbing the scaly tree trunks with sacks of fireworks on their backs. The hand-and-hook duo now perched in place, waiting for the captain's signal to begin.

Around the perimeter of the beach, Mick, Felbo, Cannonball, and the captain had made piles of Roman Candles, cherry bombs, Screaming Meemies, and firecracker strings. All was now ready. They waited also, for the right time to start the commotion.

* * *

Suddenly, the Sea Dogs watched Solo turn and go in the wrong direction. He moved toward the passel of pirates who lurched up the sandy beach. What was Solo doing, going for the third princess? They all wondered. He already had Esme. What was he up to? He was going to get himself killed!

Clyde and his men were shouting. When the Sea Dogs saw movement in the pirate camp, they knew it was time to act. Mittens and the princess had disappeared. Solo had reached the third white poodle and was struggling with her bindings. The mob of pirates had almost reached him. They shouted oaths while brandishing swords that flashed in the firelight. Some wielded heavy clubs, and some had muskets.

"Ah-oooh—ah—oooh!" Captain Rollo howled the signal and set off a string of firecrackers. On vines used as zip lines, Righty and Lefty skimmed down from the palms and tossed their packs of fireworks on the bonfire. Then they ran into the darkness, while Mick and his men rushed from one fireworks pile to the next, touching a fiery stick to each one.

Kaboom! Pow! Rat-tat-tat! The fireworks exploded in a massive wall of sound and color. As some died out, the next round began. Cannonball and Felbo covered their ears but grinned at the explosions and excitement. Captain Rollo met up with Esme and Mittens and hustled them towards the boats. Righty and Lefty surveyed the chaos and danced up and down. Mick ran out to help Solo. Spike was nowhere to be seen.

“She’s fainted,” Solo gasped as he struggled with the limp dog. He had gotten her bindings off, but they hadn’t moved away from the log.

“What are we messin’ with her for anyway, laddie?” Mick shouted, his voice almost drowned out by the noise. The advancing pirates hadn’t gotten to them yet. They were too busy jumping and dodging and running away from whizzing bottle rockets and showers of sparks. “Captain’s got the princess. They’re probably at the boats already.”

“Princess Esme insisted I save Lady Mimi, here,” Solo explained, dodging a bottle rocket himself. “She’s one of her ladies-in-waiting.”

Mick glanced at this faux princess slumped over the log. “She’s pretty—looks like Esme, she does. You sure the other's the real princess?"

Solo nodded. "Saw the birthmark. Here, grab her and let's go—we can talk later." Out of the corner of his eye, he saw a huge brown weiner dog lumbering their way, waving his sword high in the air. His yellow teeth were bared in his large face. His beady eyes glared down his long brown snout.

"Omigosh, one of the weiner dogs!" Solo shouted.

Mick hoisted the unconscious poodle easily onto his shoulders. "The same," he hissed. "This un's the the bigger and the nastier of the two. Let's go."

"Not so fast, Mick Mastiff, you scalawag," growled the pirate in a voice as ugly as he was. "You'd be takin' our property, you would."

"She ain't yours, Barbado. She's her own lady and a friend of our princess."

"That so? She'll fetch a fine ransom, then."

"She's comin' with us," Mick snarled.

"We'll see about that!" Barbado raised his weapon.

Solo swallowed hard when he saw the ugly blade hovering above him. Glancing around, he saw another big dog coming closer— he had a captain's hat on—Carbuncle Clyde!

Mick struggled to reach his sword, but he was hampered by the limp poodle draped over his shoulders. Barbado had the advantage, and he lunged toward Mick, his sword slicing the air.

Solo scooped up some sand and, clamping his eyes shut, threw it in the wiener dog's face. "C'mon Mick. NOW!"

Barbado dropped his cutlass and his hands flew to his face. "You little devil!" he howled. "I'll get you for this. I'll get you all!" He staggered blindly and fell over the log.

"Not so fast!" Carbuncle Clyde, a massive mixed-breed, shouted. He grabbed Mick's arm, the one holding the poodle. "Drop her, ye rogue."

"More sand, Solo! Get 'im!" Mick hollered as he tussled with the pirate.

Before he could even think about being afraid, Solo took up two more handfuls of sand and flung them at Clyde.

"Hah! Fooled ye!" hollered Clyde. "Closed me eyes!"

"Hah, yourself!" Solo yelled. "Take this!" He had grabbed a small log and now he swung it at Clyde's kneecaps. Direct hit! The pirate collapsed, whimpering, onto Barbado. Mick and Solo ran as fast as they could in shifting sand.

"Good work, mate," Mick heaved as he reached the crest of a dune and slipped down the other side. Lady Mimi still rested limply on his shoulders, sighing now and then if jostled too much.

"Thanks," Solo gasped, hustling his short legs along as fast as he could go. "Where's everybody else?"

"Meetin' at the boats. Got to hurry before the pirates catch up to us. This 'un needs to wake up." He gave her a gentle shake and she moaned. Now and then Solo heard a musket ball whiz by his head. His stomach lurched with every hiss of the hot lead.

* * *

There was the water. Almost home free! Solo would have broken into a four-legged run, but he didn't want to leave Mick and Lady Mimi. Heck, he might be needed. He could throw sand or wield a club again if he had to! The whizzing and exploding of the fireworks sounded farther away now and occurred with less frequency. He didn't see any pirate dogs anywhere. Good sign, he thought. He wondered where Spike was.

They reached the cove. One rowboat was almost to the Briny Belle. It must have held the princess, the captain, and the cat, for they were nowhere on shore. Felbo, Cannonball, Righty, and Lefty were jumping into the other one and preparing to shove off.

"Wait for us!" screeched Solo, hurrying ahead of Mick and Mimi.

"We're full up! Zee other boat will come back for you!" hollered Felbo. "Hey! Where's my mama's instrument?"

Solo cringed. He had completely forgotten the concertina. It was gone, gone forever. And the captain's medallion too. He'd let those two down even though he had rescued the princess. "Let us on!" he shouted. "We can't wait for the next boat; they're right behind us!"

The three of them were almost to the dinghy now. *I don't care how full up they are or how mad Felbo is*, Solo thought. *We're getting on this boat!*

Chapter Eighteen—A Salty Swim to Safety

In Solo's paws, the rough wood of the dinghy felt wonderful. It meant escape! Safety! Mick staggered up behind him, and together they handed the limp Lady Mimi off to Righty and Lefty. Gingerly, they laid her across one seat, further crowding the boat.

Felbo smiled at Solo, but the smile was not kind. "You and Meeck wait for zee other boat to come back—hide in zee water or something." When Solo tried to climb in, he pushed him back.

"No! Zee weight of you two weel swamp us and then we'll all be taken."

"By the bones of Davy Jones, you'll let us on!" yelled Mick. The whites of his eyes shone in the moonlight. *So he is afraid, too*, Solo thought. *Even the mighty Mick.*

Far from comforting him, this discovery made Solo more anxious than ever.

Cannonball tossed out two ropes. “Here! Hang on to these and paddle like crazy.”

“Yeah,” Felbo added. “Then with us rowing like mad dogs, we can make as good a time as eef you weren’t furry anchors.” He leaned right into Solo’s face. “Now shove us off and hang onto zee rope an’ pray some sharks or stingrays don’t get ya.”

Beyond the explosive din of the fireworks in the distance, the Sea Dogs heard the shouts of angry pirates. Glancing back, Solo saw the bobbing glow of torches almost at the grassy ridge where the sand began. He nudged Mick, and the two of them heaved themselves against the boat, pushing it free of the land. Twining the ropes through their paws, they plunged into the water and came up paddling.

Righty and Lefty had the oars, but Felbo and Cannonball soon edged them out of the way. With swift motions, the large black poodle and the short round pug dipped the oars into the water. They arced them through the air and back into the water again. The boat glided rapidly through the darkness.

Solo couldn’t even think about danger lurking in the black water. The noisy curses of the pirates were bad enough. Musket shots rang out, and then he heard a plop! and a hiss as the musket ball hit the water near him. Then another! And another! The boat lurched as he and Mick kicked furiously.

The Sea Dogs had pistols. Righty and Lefty stood up and fired back at the pirates.

Mick held his head up and gasped, "Don't shoot! Spike's still out there."

"Blast it! Spike can take care of himself, we say," Cannonball muttered. But the two shooters sat down.

Solo felt sick. *What was Spike doing? What had been his mission?* Solo couldn't see the Briny Belle, only the spray of water and Mick's big back rising and sinking in the water. He prayed they were almost there. His legs were tired. The brine stung his eyes. Now there were no more hisses of musket balls. *We're out of range at last. But where's the ship? Is Spike alive?*

Just when he thought he could not paddle another stroke, Solo heard a "Halloo" from somewhere. Then other voices. A scrape of wood against wood. We're safe! We did it!

He sagged with relief and the rope slipped through his paws. He was sinking like a stone and panic engulfed him, but then a strong arm grabbed him by the scruff and pulled him into the boat.

Solo coughed and spit up sea water. "Mick!" Solo gasped as he opened his eyes. "Thanks ... thanks for saving me!"

But Mick was already swaying up the rope ladder. Felbo scowled at Solo and shook the water off his foreleg.

"You ... you saved me? But I thought ..."

Felbo shrugged. "Fond of ye I ain't, but ye did rescue our preencezz. Ye be worth savin' for that." He took off his beret and held it over his heart. "Even if you deed lose my dear mama's concertina."

"I'm sorry about that, Felbo. I really am."

He pushed Solo to the ladder. "Ah! Get up there before I change my mind and toss ye back in zee water."

Being safe must be like being in heaven, Solo thought as he climbed the ladder on wobbly legs. The faces of his friends and comrades peered over the side. They cheered him onward ... Mick, Righty, Lefty, Shorty, Stretch, and the captain. It wasn't a dream then. He wouldn't wake up in his dog house with Mittens batting at his tail. They really were here, and he had really saved not only the beautiful princess but the darling Lady Mimi. *Where is Spike?* He thought. *Where is my brave friend?*

"Good work, mate!" Stretch yelled as he clasped Solo by the shoulder. "You saved the day—you and the cat. You be heroes."

The hero closed his eyes and slid out of Stretch's grasp, collapsing in a heap on the deck.

SL
MITTENS

Chapter Nineteen—Stories and Surprises

Solo awoke, pleased to feel warm and dry. The soggy sweater was gone, and the wool cap had been lost on shore somewhere. He stretched in his cozy hammock. When he opened his eyes, he saw two white poodles gazing down at him, their dark eyes full of concern. "Spike ... Spike," he tried to say, but his throat was too dry for the croak of his words to be understood.

"My dear princess, he is awake," said the first, a very pretty dog with dainty features.

"I see that, Lady Mimi," said the princess, her features also dainty though her nose was a bit longer and more pointed than the other's. *The nose of a royal*, Solo thought, and he smiled weakly.

The one he now knew as Lady Mimi had been stroking his paw, but that gentle motion stopped abruptly when he awoke. Lady Mimi flushed beneath her furry white cheeks and looked away.

Solo tried to talk but his throat was parched from all the salt water he had taken in. “A drink, please,” he rasped. He gestured toward the galley.

Princess Esme nodded to someone, and in a moment, a mug of water was in her hand. “Here. Sip this,” she said as she held it toward his mouth.

Lady Mimi helped him sit up so he could drink. The cool water slid down his throat, and he drank eagerly. “Thank you. Much better,” he said then, his voice less scratchy than before.

The boat rocked beneath them. “Are we well out to sea?” Solo asked. “Far away from the pirates?” He shuddered, recalling the angry mob cursing them at water’s edge.

“Yes, we are,” answered the princess.

Her voice is lovely, Solo thought. Like a soothing breeze.

“Is the cat okay?” he asked.

“She’s all right,” Lady Mimi said, fluffing his pillow before he settled back upon it.

“Got her tail singed a bit from a bottle rocket as we escaped,” added Princess Esme.

"Where is she? And where is Spike?"

"They are both on deck, telling their stories of what happened," answered the princess.

"Ahhhh. Spike is safe," Solo sighed with relief. "What was his mission?"

"We'll let him tell you himself," said Lady Mimi, and the princess nodded.

"Knowing Mittens, she's saying that she accomplished everything single-handedly," grumbled Solo.

"Are you feeling strong enough now to join the others?" Lady Mimi asked. "Then if she is, you can set the story straight. We both think you acted heroically."

Solo closed his eyes for a moment. Then he edged up to a sitting position in the hammock. He dangled his legs over the side and slid down to stand on his back legs. "Yeah, I'm okay," he said. "Shall we go up?" When they both nodded, he added, "Ladies first."

The white poodles smiled at each other then climbed the ladder. Solo waited discreetly until they were through the hatch and followed them.

The bracing sea air sharpened his senses. He felt alive again, refreshed and excited. Lady Mimi and Princess Esme each took one of his arms. *So this is what happens to a hero*, he thought. *I could get used to this.*

A group of Sea Dogs had gathered in a circle near the front of the ship. Everyone was there except Cannonball who had returned to the crows' nest, Captain Rollo to the helm, and Mick to the rigging to make adjustments.

Shorty and Lefty moved aside so that Solo and the two ladies had room to sit. Felbo swigged from the jug being passed around. He swiped his mouth and handed it to Spike. Shorty passed a pouch containing hard tack. Suddenly ravenous, Solo helped himself, though the two ladies declined.

"Glad to see you could make it, mate," said Mittens. She leaned back against the mast and puffed on a long, pencil-thin cigar. She leaned in to whisper something to Righty. The two of them guffawed in a cloud of smoke because Righty also had a cigar, a large, stinky one. Then they both coughed for a minute or two and slapped each other's backs.

Solo fanned the air. "Sheesh, Mittens, you never cease to surprise me. You're going to smell when we get home. What will Beth think?"

"Don' worry about it," drawled Mittens around the cigar she had stuck back in her mouth. "I'm not." She turned to Stretch who was on her other side. "As I was saying, the Princess and I ... come on over here Princess, let's tell Stretch how I almost died while saving your life."

Princess Esme smiled but remained where she was.

Solo noticed the white bandage wrapping the tip of Mittens' tail. "Humph. That doesn't look like a life-threatening injury to me, cat."

"Hurts like crazy, though. Burns do, ya know—and I'm the only one who got injured at all—'cept for him." She pointed at Spike, and then Solo saw the gauzy bandage on one of Spike's haunches.

"Teez correct," drawled Felbo, sounding even more French with some grog in him. His blue beret tilted over his good eye. "Our most succezzful meesion ever." He nodded at Spike. "Largely because of thees dog here."

"What did you do, Spike?" asked Solo. Spike grimaced as he reached back into the coil of rope he leaned on and pulled out a hand auger. He carefully tapped its vicious-looking point with a toe. "See this? It makes itty-bitty holes in wood. While you were hustling across the dunes to find the princess, I sneaked to the pirates' rowboats and went to work."

"Ah, so that's why we got away scot-free," said Solo. "I wondered why they didn't hop into their boats and overtake us. So you swam to the Belle, too?"

"I did—almost made it clear, too, except for one well-aimed musket ball that grazed my backside." Spike settled himself against the rope very gingerly. "Dang," he exclaimed. "Sabotaging the boats was the most fun I've had in years."

Solo nodded. *Fun. Well, maybe, but home is sure sounding good right now, princess or no princess beside me. I miss Beth. I miss my old, ordinary life. Being a Sea Dog is an adventure, but I it will be awhile before I choose an adventure again.*

Through the cloud of smoke, Mittens called again to the princess. "Princess Esme, please come on over and help me tell these guys what happened."

Lady Mimi cast the cat a sly look. "Are you sure the poodle you address is actually the princess?"

"Well, sure," Mittens replied as all eyes turned to Lady Mimi. "You are her lady in waiting, right? We—Solo and I—saw the dragonfly birthmark on that poodle, right there." She pointed at Princess Esme.

Mimi turned to Solo now. "Maybe I've got one, too. You didn't check under my arm."

"Huh?" exclaimed Solo, and the other dogs murmured their confusion.

"No way," coughed Mittens. "No way would the both of you have identical birthmarks, unless ..." Mittens thumped her forehead as understanding dawned.

Lady Mimi nodded. “That’s right. To fool kidnappers, we both have dragonfly marks; one, however, is a tattoo. So no one but the two of us really knows who is royalty and who is not.”

Chapter Twenty—More is Revealed

"But ... but ..." said Solo. "What do you mean, 'to fool kidnappers'?"

"Tees seemple," Felbo said. "Tees protection for our preencezz. Confused the blackguards who stole her."

Felbo's blind eye winked down at him, and Solo shivered.

"The eediots wondered wheech one was wheech," Felbo continued. "'Deed we get the right one?' they'd ask themselves, and drive each other craaazy."

"Oh, I get it," Solo responded, shaking off the sudden chill. "It bought some time until we got there to rescue them. We had to do more than storm the camp and grab the hostage—we had to figure out which one of THREE poodles was the princess."

Felbo nodded and took a sip from the jug. "That eez true ... And now we has bos of zem, safe and sound." The scruffy black poodle looked over at the two rescued ladies and fell silent.

Mittens had grown quiet also, looking from one poodle to the other. She puffed on her thin cigar. She turned back to Stretch and intoned in a very dramatic voice: "It was like this, Stretch. The sea was rough. The wind bent the palm trees almost to the ground, and in my stealth disguise, I ..."

Solo quit listening. He saw Mick taking the wheel from the captain. He waited a few moments, then excused himself from the circle. He straightened up stiffly and noticed the dark eyes of the princess and the lady—whichever was which—on him.

"Will you be all right?" asked Lady Mimi.

"Yes. It was just more swimming than I'm used to, I guess." He rubbed his stomach. "And I inhaled a bit of saltwater." He pointed toward the captain's cabin. "I just need to see the captain for a minute."

"We'll save your spot for you," said the one he knew as Princess Esme, patting the deck. "Unless we're called to breakfast. Shorty went to the galley to whip up omelets, scones with honey, and hot tea."

Solo's stomach flipped as the ship hit a swell. "Okay."

He wobbled as he made his way to the captain's cabin. *I hope he's alone. He must be because everyone else is out here or up there.* Cannonball's round head barely showed above the railing of the crow's nest, and his spyglass was trained on the eastern horizon.

The sun was almost up. The sky was now a pale yellow color tinged with pink and orange. Solo wondered how far away they were from the cove where this all began. He felt a tingle of excitement at the thought of home.

He knocked on the captain's door.

"Come in."

Solo pushed the heavy door open and went inside. "Captain Rollo, can I talk to you for a moment?"

The captain looked up from the map he had been studying. "Aye, Solo. Are ye feelin' yerself again?"

Solo moved toward the desk. "Yes, thank you. I ... I wanted to apologize for losing your medallion. I know it was very important to you."

Captain Rollo pushed back from his desk. "Aye, it was. The queen commissioned it to be made from a gold doubloon." He pointed at his chest. "For this ol' salt, himself." Then he shrugged. "Tis all right. You brought me a treasure worth more ... the princess and her companion."

Solo nodded, and then he said, "Do you know which lady is which?"

The captain's eyes narrowed as he grinned. "Oh, so they told you about the tattoo, did they?"

Solo smiled a little shyly.

"What do you think?" the captain persisted.

"Well, they're both beautiful," he said softly, "and very lady like, but I still believe that the princess is the princess and Lady Mimi is herself."

The captain looked Solo in the eye. "Does it matter to you which is which?"

Solo's gaze remained steady. "Not really. I mean, they are both fine poodles, and it's nice to get the attention. But really, I just miss my home and my simple life."

Captain Rollo relaxed. "Aye, Aye. I see. I be certain that they be who they say they be. Though it's pretty hard to tell.

"As for the medallion, I fear Carbuncle Clyde will use it gain entry in places he shouldn't. 'Tis known everywhere as mine."

Solo gulped. "I guess he can pretend he's you—but he's a different color from you, and he's bigger, too."

"Aye, that he is, but he's a clever one. He could look and act like me, easy. Did ye know, he used to be the queen's man, until he got a little greedy. Began helping himself to her jewels and such."

Solo couldn't think of a thing to say.

"We'd take plunder from pirates, and Clyde would pocket some of the best booty for himself. When the queen heard 'bout it, she coulda had him strung up but banished him instead."

"Oh. Were ... were you the one who reported him to the queen?"

"Had to. My loyalty is to the Her Majesty. Anyhow, Clyde's been my sworn enemy ever since." The captain glanced down, then looked at Solo again. "Clyde aims to do all the evil he can." He sighed. "Tries to ruin me while he's workin' his mischief."

"Sorry, sir. That he got the medallion from me, so I made it a little easier for him."

"'Tis all right, Solo. I plan to stay a jump ahead of that pirate." After a few moments of silence, the captain opened a desk drawer and pulled a crumpled wad of red cloth. It was the salt-encrusted, damp, and smelly monkey suit. He chuckled. "Say, that cat friend of yours is a wee crafty one. She earned our respect last night."

"I guess so." Praise for Mittens didn't thrill him much.

"I was going to give her this suit for a keepsake, but 'tis ruined."

Solo had an idea. “Can I take it? I want to make something for Felbo.” He explained what it was.

Captain Rollo brightened. “Get Lady Mimi to help you. She can sew.” He handed the suit to Solo.

“Okay.” Solo put the suit over his arm. “One more thing.”

The captain raised his eyes and met Solo’s gaze. “Aye?”

“We will become four-legged again when we get home, right?”

“Yes, lad, the humans won’t ken where ye’ve been, what ye’ve done, or how ye’ve moved.” He smiled, then got out of his chair. Clasping Solo in a bear hug, he said, “Glad ye joined us on our mission, laddie. Ye were as brave as ye needed to be. Did yerself proud.” Releasing him, he added, “Now go and enjoy some grub. We’ll have ye home afore the sun gets much higher.”

FELBO

Chapter Twenty-One—A Gift for Felbo

The group of dogs was no longer on the deck when Solo returned. *They must be at breakfast,* he thought. The ladies would be enjoying their scones and honey.

He'd have to catch Lady Mimi and have her make an eye patch. She sure was nice, and so was the princess.

The sun warmed Solo as he settled onto a storage box. The breeze gently ruffled his fur. Exhausted from the adventure of the night before, he let his head nod onto his chest. In a matter of moments, Solo was fast asleep. The little red suit he held slipped down to the deck floor.

* * *

Mittens happened by, carefully holding her tail upright so it wouldn't bump against anything. *No shooting pains,* please, she thought grimly. She realized that Solo was dead to the world and was tempted to jostle him awake. *It would serve him right, she thought, after enjoying the sight of me in that blasted monkey suit. I'll make it my mission to ruin his sleep for the next year or so.* She leaned down to pick up the crumpled red suit from the deck. *I can just throw this over the deck rail and never have to see it again.*

As she clasped the suit, she saw the two white poodles enter the captain's cabin. Intent on some kind of business, neither had noticed her or Solo there on the deck. Mittens was immediately curious. "What's this about?" she muttered. "Looks like a conference to me."

Dropping the monkey suit, she sneaked around the corner. She practically purred at her good luck. The captain's small window was open to let in the morning air. Sneaking closer, still mindful of her tail, Mittens stood up tall to listen. She could hear the soft murmuring of feminine voices and the deeper rasp of the captain's.

"Are you still worried about Carbuncle Clyde and his men?" asked one poodle—the princess, Mittens guessed.

"Aye. We just slowed him down, we didn't stop him." There was a pause. "'Sides, we made him mad as a cross-eyed crocodile. The scalawag'll be bent on revenge."

"Oh!" exclaimed the other poodle. Mimi. The one known as Mimi, anyway. Her voice was gentle and very quiet.

Mittens stretched up the wall of the cabin to get a little closer to the porthole. Her tail swiped against the rough wood. She gritted her teeth to keep from howling. "Dad-gum it!" she moaned as quietly as she could. She paced around in a circle until the pain subsided. Taking a deep breath, she resumed her place beneath the porthole.

"... also stole the famous robin's egg ruby that belonged to my mama ... that is, Queen Esmerelda. And, he got a whole chest of precious gems and gold doubloons."

Drat! Mittens had missed some of what had been said by Princess Esme.

"Blast that rogue!" bellowed Captain Rollo. "The queen didn't tell me that—too upset about ye, Princess." There was a pause. "I can't go back for the loot while Clyde and his gang be there. They'll have to fix their boats, but that won't take 'em long."

In the silence, Mittens could almost hear the captain thinking. "Flying flounders, I've got it. I'll send Cannonball and Felbo back to spy. Once they alert us that Clyde's crew is back in our current, we'll slip by 'em. Then we'll circle back and recover the queen's loot. Where did ye say he stashed it?"

"I didn't," was the answer. "But we both know where it is." Papers rustled. "Here, I'll draw you a map."

Mittens slumped at this news, though careful to keep her tail from touching anything. She didn't want to be a sea cat any more. And she was pretty sure Solo didn't want to sail again ... Spike, now, maybe he would, but who cared about him? It would be two against one voting NO.

"I see," said the captain. Mittens could imagine him nodding his head as he surveyed the map. "Tell you what ... Princess, ye still be in danger. Clyde might try to steal ye, again. Ye must go with Spike and Solo—both of ye."

"Will that be okay with them—and their people?"

Mittens heard the captain pacing around his desk. She imagined he'd have his hands crossed across his chest—or maybe behind his back.

"Aye. I haven't asked, but I know it'll be okay." Captain Rollo was silent a moment. "Yer Majesty, Lady Mimi ... Ye'll hide away at our landlubber friends' places...just for awhile. Ye'll be safe enough there. Clyde'd never think to hunt ye down on a farm, living like common folks."

"How will we manage that?" they asked together.

"Don't have time for a decree from the queen, so's we'll make do." the captain predicted. "The laddies admire ye both. They'll be honored to have ye as houseguests."

"Oh, dear," said the Mimi voice.

"It'll be okay, Lady Mimi. Princess," the captain answered, gently. "Now come closer, and I'll tell ye what the message will be to the queen."

The captain whispered, so Mittens couldn't hear what more was said. She pushed herself away from the wall. *Oh, brother! Two more dogs to contend with in the neighborhood? Even if they're nice, I don't want to live with them.*

She glanced at the small dog, slumbering on the cargo box a few paces away. A strange feeling constricted her chest. Could it be? An ounce of sympathy for someone she had always fought with? Mittens quickly stifled the emotion. She thought, *he better not get a crush on either of these highborn dogs. If he's that foolish, he'll be on his own—no sympathy from me.*

Chapter Twenty-Two—Getting Close

Solo drowsed in the sun. He opened one eye just as the two white poodles approached. The resemblance was so strong they could be twins.

"Hi, Solo," called the one with the longer nose—Princess Esme, Solo thought. "Did you see the captain?"

"I did. We're cool."

"Good. What's that red cloth there?" asked the other poodle. Lady Mimi. "Oh, I see, it's the suit the cat wore for our amazing rescue."

Solo nodded, picking it up from the deck. "It's damaged, though. No good as a costume any more." He looked at both dogs. "I have an idea for something sewn from a piece of this red fabric."

"Oh, tell us what it is!"

“I want to give an eye patch to Felbo, to kind of make up for losing his mama’s concertina. Can one of you stitch it up for me?”

He tossed the suit towards the females, and the one he knew as Lady Mimi caught it. “I’ll do it.”

“So you are who you say you are, I see.” Seeing their questioning looks, he added, “Cap’n said that Lady Mimi was the seamstress. Why did you have to plant the kernel of doubt about who’s who?”

Princess Esme looked at Mimi, then spoke gently. “It’s our strategy. We can’t be too careful. One never knows who can be trusted.”

“We trust you, of course,” Lady Mimi responded.

“Besides,” added the princess, “the captain thinks Carbuncle Clyde might try to steal me again. He’s sure Clyde wants revenge and a ransom in gold coin, too.”

“Captain Rollo says the stolen chest of treasure isn’t enough for Clyde,” continued Lady Mimi.

“What chest of treasure? What are you talking about?” Solo asked.

They told him what the captain had said. Solo was relieved to hear he’d get to go home. He worried a little about bringing the two poodles along. He wasn’t sure how Spike’s people would react, or his own for that matter. Beth would be okay, but the parents ... geez.

Solo drew closer to Lady Mimi. "So what about the eye patch?" he asked. "It'll have to be done right away because Cannonball is just about to shout 'Land ho!'"

"Land ho!" yelled Cannonball from the crow's nest.

"Omigosh, we just have a few minutes!" Mimi gasped as she took the ruined monkey suit. She checked it over, "Here's a piece I can use."

She started off. "I'm going to go to our cabin to make the patch," said Lady Mimi. "Are you coming, Princess?"

"Yes." To Solo she added, "We'll return in a few minutes."

* * *

Further up the deck, Spike and Mittens stood together and pointed out familiar landmarks along the rocky shoreline.

"We'll be home soon, cat," said Spike.

"Yep. And I do have a name, Spike."

"All right, Mittens." Spike turned towards her. "Do you think Solo will be okay? He swallowed so much water he almost sank."

"He'll live. He's tougher than he looks—didn't get a burn wound like I did." *Yeah, and his life is definitely going to be complicated—and yours too, you unsuspecting dog.*

Spike yawned widely and stretched his sore leg. "Oh, come on. Don't start being a baby now. You ready to go back to being four-legged?"

Mittens nodded. "Yeah. My old life has never sounded so good."

"You won't miss the adventure? The open sea? The jolly band of Sea Dogs?"

"You just said three dirty words: adventure, sea, and dogs! Make that four. Jolly. I am never going to be jolly."

She continued, "Beth will have to pry me off her bed. I'm going to sleep for a couple of weeks."

"You'll have our adventure to remember, always."

"There is that, though I never really wanted to be a swashbuckling cat. Seaview Farm, here I come."

"Nobody made you follow us down the cliff path, you know."

Mittens shrugged, then licked her front paw and awkwardly rubbed one ear. She sighed. "Shoot, it'll be a lot easier to do this when I have a normal paw again. I am so ready just to be a plain old country cat."

Spike patted the cat's back. He looked behind them at the open sea. "I know what you mean. Life on the farm will be good ... for a couple of weeks, at least. But

I think the sea's in your blood, now. You'll yearn to sail again one day."

"Hah!" was Mittens' reply.

Spike started off. "Hey, I'm going to see how Solo's doing now."

* * *

In a short while, the ship turned into Spyglass Cove. The Briny Belle dropped anchor. The captain yipped, and the Sea Dogs and sea cat assembled in front of him.

The captain looked over the animals gathered there. "Here we be. And all in fine fettle."

Mittens swished her tail three or four times. The tip of it still throbbed when she bent it too much.

"Spike, Solo, and Mittens are ready to return to their folks."

"Hoorah!" The three shouted simultaneously.

Solo raised a paw. "Um ... er ... Captain, Lady Mimi ... ah ... I ..."

"Speak up, laddie!"

"I was going to ask Lady Mimi to come to the farm with me for a vacation!" Solo blurted, beating the captain to the punch.

After a dead silence, the Sea Dogs cheered. Hats flew into the air. "Dad-burn it! This calls for some grog!" shouted Stretch. "Cheers all around."

"Hold off on the grog, just yet," Captain Rollo commanded. He stroked his chin as if pondering a new idea. Then he smiled broadly. “Aye, laddie, that will be just fine. I’m glad ye thought of it.” He winked at the small dog.

Solo smiled at Lady Mimi, not letting on that he was a bit nervous about the whole deal. She smiled back and that made it okay.

Chapter Twenty-Three—HOME!

"I tell ye what," Captain Rollo continued. "Since I'm duty-bound to go after Clyde and bring 'im in, I'd like have Princess Esme stay at yer place, Spike. Then she could rest after her run-in with that rotten pirate. And she'd be safe. The rogue wouldn't think to seek 'er out here," and his paw swept around the cove.

The captain's crew nodded and murmured their agreement with the plan.

"Spike," the captain continued, "think ye can convince your human folks to keep another dog? For a while, anyway?"

Solo and Spike looked at one another. Spike spoke first. "I don't know how I'll keep them from getting overly attached to such a beautiful dog, but ..."

He bowed, wincing only slightly because of his sore leg, and extended his fore-paw to her highness. "I would be honored to have Princess Esme as a guest at Hilltop Farm, for as long as she would like to stay. We'll manage the humans."

The princess answered demurely, "I accept the invitation. Thank you, Spike."

The cheers this time were louder than ever. The jug was uncorked and passed from Sea Dog to Sea Dog. Righty and Lefty danced a jig. Mick and Stretch slapped each other on the back. Shorty rolled on his back. Even Felbo and Cannonball were grinning.

"Thank ye, boys," the captain said. "This group, 'specially our new tars here, have made me proud. One more round, then cork the grog, Stretch. Mick and I've got to get 'em ashore and re-transform the lot."

Those going home prepared to leave the ship. Before Solo climbed down the ladder, he stopped in front of Felbo. "I know we aren't really friends, and I lost your mama's instrument, but you did pull me from the water, and I thank you for that."

Felbo said nothing.

Solo focused on the dog's milky blind eye. "Anyway, Felbo, I have two words to say to you: EYE PATCH!" And he held out the eye patch that Lady Mimi had sewn from a piece of the crumpled monkey suit.

Felbo took the patch. On one side, Mimi had stitched a short tie and on the other a long one to go around his head.

Felbo positioned the eye patch and tied it snugly into place. He set his beret at a jaunty angle and nodded at Solo. “Merci,” he said gruffly.

“Good-bye, Felbo,” he said.

“Adieu, matey.” He winked with his good eye, and Solo was relieved that the bad one was finally out of sight.

Cannonball was next in line. “You did okay, Spike. You too, Solo,” said the fat black pug. He shook their paw-hands, then pointed at Mittens. “Never thought I'd ever say it, but the cat also did okay—'bout as well as a dog.”

Mittens turned her head to hide a smile. It wasn't the best of compliments, but she'd take it—from that Sea Dog.

They said good-bye to the others on board. The five of them climbed down, one by one, into the rowboats. Mick was already in one and the captain in the other. Princess Esme waved up at the crew with her lace handkerchief. “Thank you, my loyal Sea Dogs! Don't forget me. I shall return to my mother, the queen, one day.”

“We could never forget you, preencezz!” yelled Felbo, his eye patch making him look as close to dapper as he ever would. “Someday you will be zee queen!”

The Sea Dogs hallooed them on their way.

With Mick and the captain rowing, the dinghies sped through the water. They scraped on the sand in no time at all. The dogs climbed over the gunwales and waded in to shore.

“Once again, thank ye for helpin’ save our Esme from Carbuncle Clyde.” Captain Rollo’s voice wavered as he spoke to Spike, Solo, and Mittens. “We couldn’t have done it without ye.”

He tipped his head back and closed his eyes. Opening them, he bowed low to Princess Esme and Lady Mimi. Then he turned to the others. “I might call on ye again someday soon if I need ye. A’right, maties?”

Spike immediately wagged his tail in agreement. ”Aye, aye, sir.” After a moment’s hesitation, Solo did the same. Finally, Mittens gave a slight nod of her head.

The captain smiled his long, toothy smile and said: “Well, let’s get on with the re-transformation. Then ye can head home and we’ll set sail. Ye first, yer Highness.”

“I’ll re-transform with the rest of them, if you don’t object, Captain.”

“Aye, aye. Okay by me.” He motioned for Spike, Solo, the two poodles, and Mittens to stand in a half-circle. “If you concentrate very hard, I can change ye all at once. Mick’ll help me.” He lifted his arms and made fists with his paws.

"Listen to the words. Concentrate on being four-legged again. When I am done, ye'll be just as ye were before."

After three yips and a howl, Captain Rollo and Mick waved their forelegs over the others and chanted:

"Your hands and legs have served you

well;

How you've moved no one will tell.

It's time to cast off charm and spell—

Re-join the world in which you dwell."

Solo felt strange. His limbs tingled and burned. His arms and legs twitched and his body shook. He couldn't balance. As he swayed, he saw the others through a kind of shimmering haze. They seemed spineless, too, weaving and gradually dropping to all fours.

In a few moments calm returned, and the dogs grew still. The princess, Solo, Mimi, Spike, and Mittens stood four-legged on the sand as if they had never walked on two legs at all.

Seeing that everyone had re-transformed successfully, Captain Rollo smiled at Mick and said, "Time we headed back."

"Wait!" said Solo. He had seen their collars still hanging on the branch where they had placed them just a few hours ago. "Will you fasten our collars back on us? We forgot to do that before we re-transformed." He awkwardly held up a paw. "And now we can't."

"Aye," the captain answered. He took Spike's collar and Mick took Solo's to place around their necks. By doing so, they completed the farm dogs' return to their former selves.

As Captain Rollo and Mick said good-bye to each of them, Mick paused a moment at Solo. "Ye should be proud o'yourself, matey. When I first saw ye I thought, 'there's no way that 'un will be a sailor.'" He chuckled and rubbed his forehead. "But the way you marched right into the enemy camp. Then ye stood right up to Barbado and threw sand in 'is face. That was somethin'. And got Clyde with a club, too." He clasped Solo's shoulder. "Ye made a fine Sea Dog. I'd be proud to sail with ye any time." He nodded, then turned toward the rowboat and walked away. He didn't look back

Mimi came up beside Solo. "Are you ready?"

He nodded. She trembled, and he bumped her side with his hip. "It'll be okay. You'll see."

"Are you sure your family will accept another dog?"

"They'll take to you right away." Solo tried to make a sweep with his front paw and almost fell over. "Well, I can't do that anymore," he muttered. "Besides, Mimi, we live on acres and acres of land. We have cows and a few horses. My folks can always use another watchdog." He would have crossed his toes behind his back but couldn't manage that as a four-legged dog.

"You sure you just want me to call you Mimi while you're here?" Solo asked.

"Yes, since I'm posing as a stray. The court and the world of ladies will be far away."

"I wonder what my people will call you?" Solo mused. "Beth will pick a nice name, I'm sure."

They looked over at Spike and the princess. Heads together, they were obviously working out the details of Esme's surprise appearance at Spike's farm.

Mittens hollered, "Hey, are you four coming or are you going to make plans all day long? Pardon my rudeness, Princess, but we gotta get going." Not awkward on four legs at all, the cat ran onto the steep path and started climbing.

"Mittens, I want to know," Spike remarked as the dogs caught up with her, "why you told the captain you'd sail again after you told us you were done."

"Well, what was I supposed to say with everybody staring at me, the big hero? 'Heck, no' wouldn't have cut it."

"Maybe we will go again sometime," chuckled Solo. "As long as no monkey clothes are involved. Right, Mittens?"

Mittens narrowed her eyes. "Well, DUH! I'm glad the only piece left of that suit is covering up Felbo's bad eye. Now let's get home. Come on guys, Princess, and Mimi. Once we get up over this steep part, it's clear sailing. Oh, ugh! Did I just say that?"

Soon they were at the top. They could see their farms ahead, beyond the old orchard. One last time, Solo looked down at Spyglass Cove. Mick and the captain had reached the Briny Belle. They were on board, and soon the ship would sail into open water.

Wobbling on three legs, Solo waved in case any of the Sea Dogs were looking at them. Then he turned and joined the others, hurrying home.

Made in the USA
Charleston, SC
23 February 2015